Don't Think Twice

Henry Holt and Company
New York

DON'T THINK TWICE

Ruth Pennebaker

ACKNOWLEDGMENTS

I'd like to thank my agent, Lois Wallace, for her excellent representation over the years; my editor, Marc Aronson, for being so perceptive and intelligent, as well as right an irritating number of times; and Donna McCormack for her striking cover design.

My friends have been wonderful. Thanks to Janet Foote, Deborah Little, Rebecca Marin, Katherine Sorensen, and Laurie Tranchin for reading the manuscript and encouraging me. Special thanks go to Joyce Saenz Harris, who made wonderful suggestions and should stop worrying about having a character with a similar name in the book, since the resemblance is practically nonexistent.

I'd like to acknowledge, too, the hundreds of thousands of women who have lived through situations like Anne's. They have more courage than I can imagine.

Author's note: This book takes place in 1967, before the dangers of smoking and drinking during pregnancy were well known. That's why some of the characters smoke and drink so casually.

These days doctors strongly advise expectant mothers to give up both habits.

Henry Holt and Company, Inc.
Publishers since 1866
115 West 18th Street
New York, New York 10011

Henry Holt is a registered
trademark of Henry Holt and Company, Inc.

Published in Canada by Fitzhenry & Whiteside Ltd.,
195 Allstate Parkway, Markham, Ontario L3R 4T8.

Library of Congress Cataloging-in-Publication Data
Pennebaker, Ruth.
    Don't think twice / Ruth Pennebaker
      p.   cm.
    Summary: Seventeen years old and pregnant, Anne lives with other unwed mothers in a group home in rural Texas, where she learns to be herself before giving her child up for adoption.
    [1. Pregnancy—Fiction.   2. Unmarried mothers—Fiction.   3. Adoption—Fiction.]
I. Title.   PZ7.P3846Do   1996   [Fic]—dc20   95-20499

ISBN 0-8050-4407-8

First Edition—1996

Printed in the United States of America
on acid-free paper. ∞

10   9   8   7   6   5   4   3   2   1

For Jamie

Don't Think Twice

The First Week
August 20-26, 1967

Sometimes little things depress me. My father says that's because I'm too sensitive. He says that some people are born sensitive, and I'm one of those people.

Maybe that's why I keep looking at these gingham curtains and getting depressed. I hate saggy, faded curtains. I try to look past them, but all I can see are a few trees and a lot of dust and dirt and a bright, hot sun that's burning everything up.

It's too depressing to look outside. But I don't want to look anywhere else, either. The room is just as bad.

There are two single beds that sag even more than the curtains, and quilted bedspreads you don't want to get too close to unless you like the smell of mildew. Between the beds there's a bureau. Somebody put a few small flowers in a glass of water on top of it. The flowers are supposed to be cheerful and make you feel at home. But they don't work. Nothing works.

I can hear my roommate crying every few minutes. She's trying to be quiet about it, but I notice. I notice lots of things.

She's about my age, and her name is Cheryl, "spelled with a *c-h*." She actually told me that. Maybe she thinks I can't spell. She's from Oklahoma. I know how to spell that, too: *h-i-c-k*. That's just my luck, sharing a room for four months with a farm girl. Maybe we can talk about animal husbandry when she stops crying.

I may be sensitive, but I never cry. It makes things worse when you cry. I stopped crying a long time ago, and it's worked pretty well. Sometimes I think I'm a lot stronger than I used to be. My father likes strong people. He says they're the ones who succeed. That's what I'm going to be when I get out of here—I'll be strong.

I hate to say it, but this place is a dump. There's an old black-and-white TV in the lounge. Everything looks fuzzy on it, and someone is always getting up to move the antennas around and make it look worse. The two couches are about a thousand years old, and they have shiny silver threads running through them that look very tacky. The chairs are even worse. They're old and beat up.

But that doesn't stop people from hanging around there to watch TV. They're all hard up for something to do. I'm not that hard up, fortunately. I don't like TV much. I read a lot—because it's much better for your mind. It also helps you forget things.

Today I can't forget, though. So I go outside and sit on the front-porch steps and look around. There isn't much to see. There are two cars in the parking lot that probably have an inch of dust on them, but they still reflect the sun into my face and make me wonder if you can go blind that way. Sunlight is very dangerous for your eyes.

After about ten seconds on the porch I start to sweat. I can feel it trickle down my legs. It's a million degrees and I'm sweating and I feel like I'm in prison. The only difference is, you don't have to wear stripes here. Everyone knows pregnant girls shouldn't wear stripes.

I sit on the porch and watch the wind blow through the mesquite trees and spread the dust around. I tell myself I'm going to be all right.

When I look at my watch, it's close to five. It's time to get up and go to dinner. I like to be there early so I can eat by myself and no one will bother me.

Lately I'm not sleeping well. I didn't get to sleep till almost dawn this morning, which is Tuesday, I think. About a half hour later Cheryl-with-a *c-h* gets up and starts bustling around and making a lot of racket that nobody but a dead person could sleep through. That's typical of how inconsiderate she is.

She brushes her hair into a ponytail and puts on some kind of maternity smock top. Her hair's reddish and her skin's pale, and the smock top is such a dark green that it makes her look washed out. I wonder if I should tell her she shouldn't wear that color.

She starts humming and bustling around more and then she makes her bed. "You want some help making yours, Anne?" I hear her say.

I can't believe it. She's talking to me. I wonder if I seem like the kind of person who likes to make beds. I must look even worse than I thought.

"No, thanks," I say. "I don't believe in making beds. I'm waiting for the maid to come in and change my sheets."

Cheryl seems to think I'm kidding and saying something hilarious. Some people are very easily amused. She's still laughing when she tells me she's on her way to breakfast and then to the group meeting. I wonder if she'll go there and tell everybody what a riot her new roommate is.

I don't want to hear about the group meetings. They already told me I should go to them too. Mrs. Landing stared at me through her rhinestone glasses and said, "Anne, I think it would do you a world of good to go to our meetings. The girls get together and talk about their lives and the mistakes they've made. They talk about what they plan to do after they leave here. It's good for them to talk. I think it helps."

She kept going on about how great those awful meetings were and how all the girls got to be wonderful friends. And I sat there and thought how the last thing on earth I needed was to hang around with a bunch of girls who wanted to tell how they got pregnant in the backseat of their boyfriend's car and how sorry they were that they didn't wait till they had a ring on their finger. What good was being sorry? It's too late to be sorry. That was what my father told me.

But I sat and listened to Mrs. Landing and I watched her closely, because I'd heard she had a glass eye and I was trying to figure out which eye it was. I knew then that I didn't need to go to a meeting to find out my life was a mess. Here I was in what should have been my senior year of high school. I was seventeen and I was pregnant and I was sitting on a sweaty wooden chair, listening to some woman with a glass eye. And I had to keep on listening and trying to look interested because this was the only place on earth that would have me.

It's Thursday morning, and this is how awful my life is. I get a letter from my sister and it's the high point of my day.

Mail's a big deal here. The other girls wait around for the letters and packages to be sorted, and then everybody talks about what they got. Sometimes I think they're scared everyone has forgotten them. If you get a letter, that means at least one person remembers you.

I know my mother made my sister write me. My mother likes to think we're a close family, which is a joke. My sister's jealous of me because I'm smart, and I'm jealous of her because she has blond hair (ever since she discovered Clairol) and big boobs and she got to be a cheerleader last year and she's going steady with a football player, which just about completes the whole cliché.

Her boyfriend's name is Bob. The name Bob is a palindrome. (That's a vocabulary word I learned in honors English. I may have been dumb enough to get pregnant, but I was good in English.) I told Bob that one time and he looked at me like I was crazy, but he had to be nice to me because I was his girlfriend's sister. I didn't explain what palindrome meant. He probably thought it was a horse like Trigger.

The minute I see the letter, I know it's from Pamela. She uses garish, hot-pink stationery and she has childish handwriting. She doesn't dot her *i*'s with circles anymore, ever since I'd pointed out the similarity between the circles and her IQ.

I can't see myself standing around with all the other girls, reading some of the letter out loud and talking and laughing. So I take the hot-pink letter back to my room and sit on the bed and open it. Right away the air fills up with some kind of perfume. Tigress, I guess. I try to figure out why Pamela is wasting perfectly good perfume on me. Maybe Bob's been sent to a state school for good-looking retarded people and she's getting desperate.

Anyway, here's what she wrote.

Dear Anne,

Hi! School started today and I've allready got loads of homework. My hardest class is geometry, but the teacher is a football coach that's young and cute, so I bet I'll do alright. We've started cheerleading practice and I'm worn out. Maggie Scott has gained at least twenty pounds and looks awful. I think they should make a rule about cheerleaders weight. Its embarrassing to have her on the squad.

Bob and I went to an end of the summer dance on Saturday. Jake was there, I think with a sophomore. He said hi and I said hi and that was all. He acted a little funny, but that was ok.

Well, I have to hit the books. You're lucky you don't have to!

Love ya,
Pammie

I sit and study the letter. I try to figure out why Pamela spells *already* with two *l*'s and *all right* with one *l*. Also, hasn't she heard of apostrophes? Maybe she didn't get enough oxygen at birth. That would explain a few things.

I wish I hadn't read her stupid letter. I don't want to hear about school and I don't want to hear that I'm lucky I don't have to study and I sure as hell don't want to hear about some dance she went to. Just reading the letter makes me feel terrible. Pamela's life hasn't changed a bit. Everything's the same for her.

My father always said I was supposed to be a good example for Pamela since I was two years older and a lot smarter. Every time I made the honor roll, he asked her why she didn't. That's another reason why she hates me. "Anne's going to be a success someday," I heard him tell her one time. "And at the rate you're going, you're not." Pamela started crying after he said that, and she didn't speak to me for about a month. She's sensitive and petty about things like that.

I know I shouldn't have eavesdropped on them, but that's one of my bad habits. I have lots of bad habits. Or maybe I just have a bad personality.

The point is, eavesdropping is interesting. You can hear secrets that way, especially at our house. A month ago I heard my father tell my mother that I was still an example for Pamela. I knew when he said it that I was a different kind of example these days. I was a negative example. Pamela could look at me and see how I'd done something terrible and humiliated my whole family and how nobody in her right mind would want to be like me.

When I heard my father say that, I thought I was sneaking around, hearing something interesting that I wasn't supposed to hear. Now I think he wanted me to hear, because he knew how terrible it would make me feel. He was right, too. He understands me. He's very smart about people.

I crumple Pamela's letter into a hot-pink ball and throw it against the wall. I feel a funny pain move from my heart to my stomach and back again. These days everything is making me sick.

The Second Week
August 27-September 2

It's Sunday, and everyone's at a movie. I could have gone. Mrs. Landing said it would do me some good to get out and forget about all my problems. I wanted to say, "What problems, Mrs. Landing? Everything's fine in my life."

But I didn't say that. I wasn't feeling mean enough. I told her that I needed to stay here and write my sister a long letter. She looked happy to hear me say that, like I was close to my sister and wanted to keep in touch. ("Your family may be disappointed in you, but they still love you very much," she told me last week. "You're fortunate to come from a family that cares about you." When she said that, it made me wonder how many hundreds of girls she'd said that to, and whether anyone had believed her.)

It's too quiet with everyone gone. I don't like it when it's noisy, and I don't like it when it's quiet like this, and that makes me think I don't like anything these days, which is pretty accurate.

So I crawl back into bed and I lie there, under the sheet. Sometimes I feel my stomach through it. Even though I'm lying on my back, it still sticks out. It's growing a little every day. I can't understand it. How can this be happening to me? How can my body be changing so much—and there's nothing I can do about it?

When I saw the doctor, he gave me a pamphlet about pregnancy. There were pictures in it that showed how a fetus grows. Right now, it's small and it looks like a shrimp with a big head. It's about the size of my hand. That's not very big, but it's already changed my whole life. It isn't a baby, really. It's more like a tumor, and it's poisoning everything.

I've heard about women who throw themselves down a bunch of stairs so they'll have miscarriages. I'd love to throw myself down some stairs or out a window. I wouldn't care if I killed myself doing it. Or maybe if I hurt myself badly enough, then I wouldn't feel anything for a long time. I'd just step off a high point and for a few wonderful seconds, I'd be floating and I wouldn't feel a thing.

Mrs. Landing is worried about me. She says I spend too much time by myself.

It's early in the evening, and she's come to my room to tell me that. She sits on my bed and starts to talk and talk. She says things like how all of us are in the same boat and we should help each other. "You need to make friends with the other girls, Anne," she says.

As usual, once she starts, she goes on talking forever. Cheryl's sitting on her own bed, pretending to read a paperback book without a cover. I glance at her to see if she's moving her lips while she reads it. She isn't, so she must be eavesdropping.

What do I care? All I can do is think about the picture of all of us being in the same boat. It looks like some kind of leaky Noah's Ark, with all of us poor, unmarried pregnant girls on it. It goes out to the deepest water, where it sinks from its own illegitimate weight. People gather on the shore and watch it sink. They hear the screams, but they don't do anything.

It's quieter in the room now, and I notice that Mrs. Landing has stopped talking. She's looking at me. I can tell she wants me to say something. She probably wants me to cry, so she can tell I'm normal and she and Cheryl can comfort me. But I don't feel sad and I don't feel like crying. I just want everything in my life to be different, and I know it isn't going to be.

I stare at my hands, which are clenched shut. I stare at Mrs. Landing's red-and-white floral dress until it starts to disappear. I stare at our room, which looks like the inside of a shoe box. The silence drags on, and I know I'm supposed to break it. I know what Mrs. Landing wants me to say, and finally I say it.

"Okay," I whisper. "I'll come to the meeting tomorrow."

That seems to make her happy, even though I can tell

she's thinking I don't have the right attitude yet. She pats me on my hands and smiles.

After she leaves, I lie back on my pillow. Cheryl's still reading and doesn't say anything. I glance at her every few minutes, and one time I'm sure I caught her moving her lips.

I'm a very weak person. I swore over and over that I'd never go to one of those meetings. I've only been here a week, and I've already given in. The next thing you know, I'll be knitting baby booties like some of the other girls.

When I was in the bathroom yesterday, I heard a girl talking about something that happened here last year. One of the girls tried to abort her baby by sticking a knitting needle up herself. She bled all over the place and they took her to the hospital and no one saw her again. Ever since I heard that story, I think about that girl every time I see someone knitting. I always wonder if they threw out the knitting needle she used or if they just washed it off and gave it to someone else.

I'm going to the meeting because I told Mrs. Landing I would, even though I know it's a dumb idea. The group meetings are held every weekday at ten, and they're supposed to last an hour. Mrs. Landing said that sometimes the meetings are so interesting they go on lots longer though. I nodded when she told me that. I'm very good at nodding when people say dopey, unbelievable things.

Everyone's gathered in a small room at the end of the hall. The room has only one window and there aren't any curtains on it, so you can enjoy the bad view.

Mrs. Landing has us pull our chairs together in a lop-sided circle. There are eight of us, counting her. Cheryl's here, of course. She goes to these meetings every day, and she also goes to some kind of Bible study group every morning. She must love all those meetings, because she looks a lot more cheerful these days, and she goes around humming pretty loudly all the time. That gets on my nerves.

Harriet is here too. She's from Kansas or one of those other midwestern states I always get confused, since they all look alike. She's one of Cheryl's Bible-thumping friends, and most of the time she goes around clutching a white leather Bible with her name printed on it in fake-gold ink. Harriet's hair is almost white, and she's very wispy looking. Even her glasses look wispy.

There's another girl who's about twelve or thirteen. Her name is Gracie. She was raped by her father. I heard that in the bathroom too. The only way I find out inter-esting things is when I eavesdrop. I don't have anything better to do, though.

The other girls look vaguely familiar. They're all about my age, but they're bigger than I am. More pregnant, I mean. I can tell by looking at them that we don't have anything in common, except bad luck. That's all right, though. I'm not here to make friends. I don't need friends as much as most people do. I'm used to being by myself.

Since this is my first meeting, Mrs. Landing asks me to introduce myself. The way she says it reminds me of being in school the first day of classes. Except in school everything is new and exciting and fresh, and maybe wonderful things will happen to you. Unlike this place, where all you do is wonder how much worse it will get.

I can tell that Mrs. Landing has already talked to everyone about me and told them I'm a problem case, because they all look at me and act interested. Even Cheryl, who already knows me, kind of.

"My name's Anne, and I'm from Texas," I say. We aren't supposed to use our last names here. "I'm from Dallas. There's nothing else to tell. I guess I'm here for the same reason everyone else is."

I don't know why I said that. I'm always saying stupid things. Maybe I thought it would sound funny, but it doesn't come out that way. Two or three of the girls look embarrassed, and I can't tell if they're feeling bad for themselves or for me. Cheryl's hands are folded in her lap, and she's staring down at them. Some friend. No wonder I never try to talk to her.

Mrs. Landing is speaking now. That must be her idea of a group meeting, for her to do all the talking.

"What we do in this group, Anne," she says, "is to try to talk about how we feel about being here. I know it's hard for you. It's been hard for all the girls. But you have to work at it. You have to try to get that chip off your shoulder. There are girls here who'll be your friends if you'll let them."

She looks at me. As usual I can tell she wants me to say something. And as usual I'm disappointing her. But I don't feel like saying anything more. I'm tired of hearing that I have problems and a chip on my shoulder and a bad attitude. Of course I do! My life is terrible, and it's not going to get any better.

I hunch over and cross my arms in front of my stomach. It's getting bigger every day. My stomach is getting bigger and every other part of me is shrinking.

I sit like that for the rest of the meeting. When it's over, I realize I haven't heard a word that anyone has said.

For the rest of the week, I refuse to go to any more meetings. Whenever Cheryl asks me about it, I tell her I'm not feeling well. I can tell she doesn't believe me, but she's too polite to say so. I wonder if the rest of them will talk about me since I'm not there. Let them. It will keep their minds off their own problems, which, I'm sure, are as bad as mine.

At least I know I have problems. I give myself points for that. It's about the only thing I give myself points for these days.

Besides, there's something I have to do this morning. It's already Friday, and last week I got a letter from my mother. I walked back to my room and put it on the night table next to my bed. I didn't want to open it. I still don't, but I know I have to.

I can tell what my mother's doing. She's trying to stagger the family's letters. First she made Pamela write me. (She probably had to threaten to withhold peroxide or something drastic like that to get Pamela to sit down and write.) Then, a few days later, she wrote me herself. I'm sure I can expect something from my father soon. "Be positive," my mother will tell him. "She needs our support now."

And that's the problem. I don't want the kind of support she wants to give me.

My mother is one of those very religious people who goes to church three times a week. She even sings, quite badly, in the church choir. As far as she's concerned I've sinned and I've gotten exactly what I deserved, which is getting pregnant. I know she's embarrassed and ashamed of me. But in some funny corner of my mind, I know my mother even better than that. I know she's pleased I've gotten my comeuppance.

I'd been my father's favorite, and I'd thought I was smart and that I was going places. For years I'd known my mother hated me for that. I knew she loved me, but she hated me, too. I'd seen it in her eyes and heard it in her voice. Sometimes she even said it out loud. "You're not as smart as you think you are," she said once when I told her I wanted to be a writer and live in New York City. "You don't know how hard it is to succeed. Most people never get what they want. You'll find that out someday."

Well, I guess she was right. I'd gotten pregnant, and that someday she was talking about has arrived. I'm not going to get what I want. The life I planned on is over. And now she wants to comfort me for finding that out.

All of my striving and my big-headed ideas are behind us now. By getting pregnant, I broke my father's heart. But in some kind of way, I know I made my mother happy. Now she can feel sorry for me and take care of me. Now she knows I won't do any better with my life than she's done with hers. All of this has made her love me, really, for the first time in years.

I know what's in her letter. It's full of pity and forgiveness and fake good cheer. She's welcoming me back, taking me back as her daughter. That's what this is all about. That's what the letter is.

I put the letter in the nightstand drawer and close it. The more I think about it, the more I realize there's no reason to read it.

The Third Week
September 3-9

It's Monday, and I'm going back to the group meeting. Mrs. Landing told me I don't have to talk if I don't want to. She just wants me to be there, she said.

So here I am. Mrs. Landing opened the window in the room, and you can feel a sticky breeze sometimes that makes you even hotter. I guess she figured that out, because she also brought in one of those rotating fans. Every few minutes it blasts you in the face and makes your hair stick to your sweaty cheeks.

Maybe they've never heard of air-conditioning out here in the country. This is typical summer weather for Texas, and it's going to be steaming hot for another month or two. By November you might be able to breathe again without wanting to die.

I glance around the circle and count the knitters.

There are two today. Harriet is one of them. She's knitting something pink. It's only about an inch long, but you can tell she doesn't have much future as a knitter. The stitches are so droopy you could drive a truck through them. As usual Harriet has her Bible with her, propped on her lap. I guess she never knows when she might want to read about God's smiting somebody. I love that word, *smite*.

When the meeting starts, I don't say a word. Neither does Cheryl or Gracie. Gracie never says anything. She never even looks at anyone else. She always sits and hugs her stomach and stares down at the floor. It makes me wonder why she bothers to come to these stupid meetings. She could look at the floor in her own room. There's the same ugly linoleum in every room. No wonder Gracie looks so sad and scared all the time. Staring at that floor would make anybody feel worse.

Donna is the first one to talk. She has short, straight brown hair and dark eyes. I have the feeling she's the kind of girl people refer to as "perky." But you wouldn't call her perky right now. Crazy is more like it. She jumps right in and starts talking about how much she still loves her boyfriend.

"Some of you have heard this all before," she says. She's kind of apologetic, but she doesn't stop talking. "But Dick and I have been together forever. I mean, we've been going together since the seventh grade, and we've always loved each other. I've thought about it a lot, and I don't think the baby could make him stop loving me."

Donna has a handkerchief in her hands, and she keeps twisting it around while she talks. The longer she talks, the more she twists it. "Dick still loves me," she says. "I know he still loves me. And he's going to love the baby, too. It's just taking him time to realize that. I know it must seem strange to everybody that we're apart right now. But it's temporary. We're going to be back together soon."

I feel sick all of a sudden. I don't think I can listen to Donna for another minute. How can she go on talking like this? Why doesn't she just rip her heart out right here in front of everybody, as long as she's at it? Is she about to have a nervous breakdown? (If so, I want to leave and go read a book. My mother had two nervous breakdowns, and I don't like being around them. They make me very twitchy.)

I can't put my hands over my ears, because that would be too obvious. So I start thinking about anything, just to keep my mind occupied. That way I don't have to listen to Donna.

I think about their names. Donna and Dick, Dick and Donna. That sounds like the name of a singing group. Maybe they're one of those awful folk groups that writes their own music. Great. Donna is probably the type who brought her guitar to the home because music means so much to her, she can't live without it. She probably sits around and composes lovesick songs. I'm sure she'll start coming to all our rooms, begging us to help her come up with words that rhyme with "Dick" and "brokenhearted" and "stretch marks." We'll have to start locking our doors to keep her out.

I can hear some of the other girls talking now. That's a good sign. That's very promising. Maybe Donna isn't going to crack up after all. Or maybe she can wait till I go back to my room and stuff cotton in my ears.

The other girls are asking Donna questions, and she's answering. "No," she says, "I haven't heard from Dick in several weeks. But that doesn't mean he doesn't love me. It just means he's going through a hard time right now."

She bends her head a little and stares at her handkerchief. "I did hear he was dating someone else," she whispers. "Someone told me that."

She looks up and starts talking in a louder voice. "But I don't believe it. I know he still loves me. I think it's all going to work out—I mean, I know it is. He's going to realize how much he loves me and we'll get married and we'll keep the baby."

Donna draws a big, loud breath. "I can hope, can't I?" she says. "It's better to hope, isn't it?" Her words hang in the air, like a bunch of tattered laundry. No one says anything, so she answers her own question. "Yes, it's much better to hope. I know that. It's always better to hope."

By now she's crying, but she keeps trying to smile, too. That's the worst part. I watch a tear slide down her cheek onto her dress. I shut my eyes but I can still see her, crying and trying to smile.

Finally everything is quiet. Donna's stopped talking.

She rests her head on her hand and stares at the floor. Her face is tired and sad, and I try not to look at her.

The meeting must be over. Thank God. I want to run to my room and lock the door and refuse to let anyone in. I'll never come out again—never. They'll have to drag me out by force, and I'll scream all the way.

But then LaNelle starts talking. Wonderful. Just wonderful. I get depressed every time I look at LaNelle. She has brown hair and a freckled face, and she talks in a mountain drawl that's so bad it makes Cheryl sound like the Queen of England. Her eyes are always red, like she's just finished crying or she's about to start.

"I'd always known it was the best thing to give up my baby," LaNelle says. "I didn't have any doubts. My family's real poor. There's no way they could afford to feed another child. Besides, my dad's got problems. He beat me bad when he found out I was pregnant. I couldn't think what he'd do to a little baby. But—" LaNelle keeps saying that word, *but,* like it has about five syllables. "But now, I'm thinking more and more about the baby. I can feel it move every day, and I feel like I know it. And sometimes I think I can't bear to give it up and never know where it lives or what it's doing.

"How can I do that?" She starts to cry. The girl sitting next to her passes a handkerchief. "How can I give up my baby?" LaNelle says. "How can I?"

She's sobbing now, and her face is red and blotchy. The girls on either side of her have their arms around her. I look slowly around the circle and see that everyone else looks almost as bad as LaNelle. Cheryl is about to burst into tears. Even Harriet has stopped knitting and is clutching her Bible like it's a sponge she's trying to wring out.

Somewhere inside, I can feel a part of me begin to ache. I don't want to feel that. I don't want to feel anything. It's too dangerous. If I let myself feel anything, it will never end. I can't let it start.

You've got to stop it! That's what I want to tell Donna and LaNelle. You've got to stop it! You're asking questions and saying things that are worthless. You're only hurting yourselves and making everything worse.

Everything in me wants to tell Donna to forget all about Dick. She'll never see him again, and they'll never be together. And she's completely wrong about hope. It's always worse to hope, always. Hoping for something breaks your heart.

As for LaNelle, I want to tell her that it's better never to think about her baby. She should never think about keeping it, either. It would be so much easier for her to think of pregnancy the way I do. There's a growth inside me, and in a few months it will come out. And I'll leave here and it will all be over and I'll never think twice about it. That's what my mother told me. We'll never talk about any of this again. It will be over and our lives will go on. Everything will be the same.

I want to say all of this, but I can't. These are things I can't bear to think about or talk about, now or ever. My life is bad enough already, and there's no reason to make it worse. If LaNelle or Donna asks me what I think, I'll tell them. But they don't ask me. So all I can do is sit here and wait for everybody to stop crying.

On Wednesday I get a letter from my father. I know it can't be as bad as anything that my mother's written, so I open it.

My father wrote that everything was fine. He won a big case last week. It had to do with an insurance company and subrogation. He played golf twice at the club. The weather was still hot. He was well. My mother was well. Pamela wasn't spending enough time on her schoolwork, as usual. But she was well too. He hoped that I was well.

That's it. He signed the letter, "Love, Daddy." I count the number of lines in the letter. Twenty-four. I wonder how long it took him to write it. I wonder what he thought about when he wrote it. Except for the ending, it could have been a letter to a client or a total stranger.

I stare at the letter for a while and think about my father. He looks younger than most of my friends' fathers. He has thick brown hair and eyes that are almost black. There's something unusual about his eyes. When I was little, I used to think his eyes could see everything. It wasn't like X-ray eyes in the comic books, where people could just see objects. I always thought my father could see inside people and understand them. He seemed to know so much about everything and everybody. Everyone always said how smart he was and how good looking and successful.

I felt proud when I heard people say that. I felt proud to have a father like him and to have him love me so much.

That's why hurting my father was one of the worst things about my getting pregnant. It made me sick to think about what I'd done. I knew I'd broken Daddy's heart.

That's what my mother told me. A few times she said, "You've broken all our hearts." But mostly she told me I'd broken my father's heart.

I believed it then, but now I don't believe it anymore. I look at what my father wrote and what he didn't write, and I don't see a letter from someone whose heart is broken. It's a letter from someone whose heart is just fine. He healed himself and went on without me. Maybe he had always been like that, and I hadn't realized it.

Tuesday and Thursday nights Cheryl and I wash dishes. Mrs. Landing says that doing chores is part of being at the home. She acts like washing dishes is going to build my character and make me a wonderful person. I'm pretty sure it's a violation of child-labor laws, since I'm only seventeen. I'm thinking about writing my congressman, except I don't know who he is.

I haven't complained to Mrs. Landing, though. I'm afraid she might stick me with Harriet, cleaning the bathrooms. Harriet would probably start reading her Bible out loud and witnessing to me, and then I'd have to stick my head down the toilet and flush a lot so I couldn't hear her.

Compared with that, washing dishes isn't so bad. Sometimes Cheryl and I talk a little. But usually I concentrate on the dishes and scrub as hard as I can, and sometimes that makes me feel better. I can let my mind wander.

Thursday night I got a great idea while we were washing the dishes. It's a new strategy to survive this place. I'm going to go to those group meetings and watch them like they're a soap opera. The other girls will be the actors and I'll be the audience. I'll let Gracie be in the audience too. Or maybe she'll be a prop. I haven't decided yet.

LaNelle will be the main character, which is too bad. Soap operas should have more attractive heroines who say interesting things. Maybe they'll get some new writers who'll realize what a problem LaNelle is, and they'll get rid of her. Soap operas are like that. I know, because my mother watches lots of soap operas. Characters are always getting run over by tractor-trailers or dying from some terrible disease. If I were writing the soap opera, I'd give LaNelle lockjaw.

But I'm not writing it. I'm just in the audience. So here I am Friday morning, sitting through another meeting and listening to LaNelle and sometimes Donna, but mostly LaNelle. I wonder if there's some kind of rule going on here. Maybe the one who's the most pregnant always does the most talking.

Thanks to all these meetings I go to, I now know everything about LaNelle. I know more about LaNelle than I know about myself. I know she's from Arkansas and she's the oldest of seven kids and she loves children and her father is some kind of lowlife worm who beats them all with a razor strap "for their own good." He drinks too much and he has a terrible temper, and LaNelle is scared to death of him.

LaNelle says her boyfriend wanted to marry her, which I find hard to believe. "But I knew that would be a mistake," she says. "You know, I don't want to end up like my mama. She's not that old—she's not even forty. But she looks so old and tired and worn out by having so many children.

"I know it sounds like bragging. But I wanted to make something better out of myself. I thought maybe I could take classes at one of the junior colleges. Sometimes people do that and then they can transfer to a university. That's what I've been planning on. That's why I was going to give up the baby. I just never thought how much it would hurt."

The meeting wears on and LaNelle keeps talking and crying as usual, and hogging the conversation with stuff everyone's heard at least a hundred times. I look at my watch and notice she's been talking for more than an hour.

I wonder why Mrs. Landing never does anything about that. She always sits and listens and nods sometimes, as if all of this is fascinating. Sometimes I wonder if she's listening or if she's just learned to sleep with her eyes open.

Finally LaNelle stops talking. She looks exhausted and even worse than usual. No one else says anything. I mean, what can anybody say?

Then I remember that I planned to watch this like a soap opera. Damn. I forgot all about it.

I'm not really here, I try to remind myself. I'm not a part of any of this. I'm only watching it, remember? I'm thousands of miles away from all these people, and even if I reached out my hand, I couldn't touch any of them. I have to remember that.

The Fourth Week
September 10-16

We're all awakened before dawn on Sunday. Someone is screaming.

I jump out of bed and open the door. Cheryl's right behind me, pulling on her robe. All the other girls are out in the hall too, looking sleepy and scared.

Donna is standing a few feet away, outside the room she shares with LaNelle. Their door is closed.

"LaNelle's in labor," she says. For some reason she's whispering. Her hair is all messed up and she looks nervous. "Mrs. Landing's in there with her," she says. "They're sending an ambulance from the hospital."

Another scream. This one is worse. It rakes through the air and seems to last forever. I want to put my hands over my ears and run somewhere, but I can't move. I stay in the hall with everyone else. We're all quiet and still, like shadows.

I can hear the shrill sound of a siren in the distance, coming closer. It gets louder and louder, and then it stops. The outside doors bang open, and I can see two men in white walking down the hall. Between them they're pulling some kind of bed on wheels. I wonder why they're not running. It's an emergency, isn't it? They're strolling, practically. They both have white, puffy faces and they look like the village idiots. It's a miracle they can walk upright.

LaNelle's door opens and Mrs. Landing comes out. She looks calm. I'm relieved there's someone around here with an IQ over twenty-five who looks calm. I feel like a wreck. Every time I hear another scream, I almost pass out.

"She's in there," she tells the two men, gesturing. "She's bleeding and she's in terrible pain. You need to hurry." Mrs. Landing sounds like she knows what she's doing. Even the two idiots listen to her.

Of course she knows what she's doing, I realize finally. She's been through all of this before. I don't want to think how many times.

We all move back farther from LaNelle's door. I can hear noises from her room as the men put her on the bed. She isn't screaming any longer. Maybe they've given her something for the pain. But she's whimpering and moaning, terrible sounds that seem to dig into my skin.

The two men push her out of the room and into the hall. Mrs. Landing follows them. "I'm going to ride in the back with her," she tells the men. "She needs someone with her."

They move quickly past all of us. I don't want to look at LaNelle, but I can't help it. She's lying on the bed under a sheet. I hardly recognize her. Her face looks frozen and white, like some kind of horrible mask. I wish I hadn't looked at her, because I keep seeing her face.

This is what it's like, I think. This is what childbirth is like. It looks horrible and scary, like LaNelle's face and her screams. This is what's going to happen to me and everyone else in this hall. This is what I can expect in another three months. I keep telling myself that, but I don't believe it.

The doors bang shut. A few minutes later the siren blares. We all jump a little and stare at each other. Gradually the siren gets softer and softer as it moves back into the distance. In the hall it's quiet again. All I can hear are a few birds chirping outside, and I realize the sun is coming up.

It's Sunday night when we hear that LaNelle's baby died. LaNelle is going to be all right, but her baby is dead.

Mrs. Landing comes into the dining room to tell us. She looks tired and old. Even her voice seems tired.

"LaNelle lost a lot of blood," she says. "But she's young and strong, and she's going to be fine. The baby . . . the baby wasn't premature, but its lungs weren't developed. It was . . . it was one of those things. The doctors didn't know why."

Her voice trails off. No one says anything.

Mrs. Landing clears her throat. "It lived for three hours," she says, "until nine o'clock this morning, and then it died. It didn't suffer. I know that. Maybe it was for the best."

Everything is so quiet. There isn't a sound. I keep wishing for a noise from somewhere, anywhere. I hate this kind of quiet. I can't breathe when it's this quiet.

"You'll have to excuse me," Mrs. Landing tells us. "But I must get to bed. I'm not going to be any good to anyone if I don't get some sleep."

She leaves slowly, and we hear her footsteps going down the hall. Her bedroom is at the far end, next to the outside door. We hear her door close. Once again it's completely silent. Even when we all get up and take our trays to the dishwashing area, you can't hear much of anything.

I can't figure it out. I don't know why I feel so terrible.

I hadn't even liked LaNelle. I'd been sick of her belly-aching about giving up her baby. I'd thought she was almost as crazy as Donna, with her nutty ideas about getting together with her boyfriend and getting married and having the baby and living happily ever after.

So why am I feeling so awful about her and the baby? Nobody wanted that baby. It was a mistake from the beginning. What difference does it make that the baby died? LaNelle would have given her up! It wouldn't have been hers, anyway. It would have belonged to someone else. It would have been taken away from her, and she would have gone for the rest of her life without ever seeing it or knowing whether it lived or died. So why does the baby's death make such a big difference? Why does it matter so much? Why does it matter so much to me?

Mrs. Landing says it's for the best. She's right, isn't she? The baby's death is for the best.

At the group meeting Donna brings up all of this. Her cheeks are bright red and she looks furious. She may be going crazy again.

"I'd like to know more about LaNelle's baby," she says to Mrs. Landing. "You keep calling the baby 'it.' I want to know if it was a boy or a girl. I want to know if it had a name."

Mrs. Landing is about to speak when Donna starts talking again. She looks even angrier now. "I want to tell you something else, too," she says. "I think what you said about the baby's death being for the best was absolute shit. LaNelle loved that baby. How can you say its death was for the best? That's a lie, and you know it."

I've never heard anybody my age talk like that to an adult. I'm amazed. I wonder if Mrs. Landing will make Donna wash her mouth out with soap. Maybe she'll kick her out of the home or put her in an institution.

Mrs. Landing doesn't say anything for a few minutes. She sits and stares at her hands, which are folded in her lap. I'm sure she's trying to think of a good way to get rid of Donna without making a big fuss.

Finally she nods. "You're right," she says. Her voice is low, and it sounds strange. "You're right, Donna. Nothing that happened at that hospital was for the best. Nothing.

"The baby was a girl, and she was perfectly beautiful.

She was pink and bald-headed and lovely. After she was born, LaNelle got to see her. She got to touch her and talk to her before she died. She told me she wanted to name her Laurie. That was a name she'd always liked."

Mrs. Landing falls silent for a few more seconds. "I think it was one of the saddest things I've ever seen," she says. "I can't tell you how sad it was to be there and to watch it. It broke my heart. That's why I didn't want to talk about it much."

She looks slowly around the circle, from face to face. "I'm sorry," she says.

On Wednesday we hear there's a new girl at the home. I guess that's how things are at this place. One girl leaves and another comes and a baby dies and everything goes on and we aren't supposed to notice the difference. This place is like some kind of lazy Susan. It's very emotionally unhealthy.

The first time I see the new girl, I hate her. Her name is Nancy and she's from Mississippi and she looks like a blonder version of my sister, which means she has a serious peroxide habit. She's also an extrovert, just like Pamela. If there's anything I hate, it's an extrovert.

Five minutes after Nancy introduces herself to the group, she tries to take it over. She acts like she's been here forever. That irritates me. Who does she think she is? She doesn't know a thing about any of us. Maybe she has this place confused with her sorority house. The next thing we know, she'll be suggesting that we all wear sweatshirts with the name of the home on them, and we'll have sing-alongs and Donna will play her guitar.

To hear Nancy talk—which we do, believe me—she's the most popular coed in the history of the University of Mississippi. Some nights she even had two dates, she says with a big white grin. She has great teeth. I can tell she knows it, too.

"Some of my sorority sisters were so jealous, they wanted to kill me," she says.

What stopped them? I wonder.

An hour passes, and Nancy isn't showing any signs of shutting up. But Mrs. Landing says it's time for us to stop anyway. "We'll have plenty of time to continue to get to know each other, Nancy," she says. She seems a little irritated at Nancy, but I'm probably imagining it.

After the meeting's over, I walk down the hall with Cheryl, back to our room. "I think someone should gag that Nancy and push her off the roof," I say.

As soon as I say that, I wish I hadn't. Why did I open my mouth? Cheryl and all her Bible-thumping friends never say anything mean about anybody. They're always trying to be fair and pious and high-minded. They make a big deal about trying to find the good in everyone.

Unlike me. Completely unlike me. I have a bloodhound's nose for the bad in everyone.

"Oh, I don't know," Cheryl says. "I'm not sure the roof's high enough."

A day later LaNelle's father comes to get her things. He isn't at all what I expected.

I thought he'd be about ten feet tall and mean looking and scary, like some kind of hillbilly Dracula. But he isn't. He's small and slight and he walks a little bent over. He's taken off his hat, and he's calling everyone—including us—"ma'am." His accent is even worse than LaNelle's.

Mrs. Landing already told us that LaNelle wouldn't be coming back here to see us. "She said it would remind her of too many things," she said. "She just wants to leave town and forget." The baby's going to be buried somewhere in Arkansas, Mrs. Landing said. LaNelle wanted Laurie close by so she could visit her grave.

Donna had stacked LaNelle's two suitcases outside their door for LaNelle's father to take. On top of them she'd folded a homemade quilt LaNelle brought with her. The quilt is torn on one of its corners, and stuffing is coming out of some of the squares. I wonder if it was already torn or if LaNelle ripped it somehow when she went into labor.

LaNelle's father picks up the two suitcases and drapes the quilt over his shoulder. "Good-bye, ma'am," he says to Mrs. Landing. He shakes her hand very seriously. "I just want to get my girl home now. She'll get better, being at home."

I watch him closely and try to find something in his sunburned face. I'm trying to catch a glimpse of the man who beats his wife and children, and drinks and goes into sudden rages. I'm good at things like that, at seeing people, like my father is.

I know all about LaNelle's father and I want to see

him up close. But when I look at him, his face is a stranger's.

At our group meeting on Friday, Nancy starts holding court once again. I've now decided she's a deeply superficial person.

For one thing, she's complaining about how terrible maternity clothes are. "I've always been well dressed," she says. "It's important to me. But maternity clothes! I can't find a thing that I like! Can you believe how bad they are? There's nothing out there that's flattering, even for me."

Nancy laughs when she says that, like she's saying something hilarious. She must think her maternity fashion commentary is very insightful and witty. It probably would have them rolling in the aisles back in Mississippi. It has me rolling my eyes.

Not that Nancy notices. As far as I can tell, the world's a mirror for her. She makes my sister, Pamela, seem like Eleanor Roosevelt. (Which is strange to think about, since I doubt Pamela's ever heard of Eleanor Roosevelt. I'll have to ask her someday. I'll tell her Eleanor is a famous cheerleader for the UN. That will pique Pamela's interest. She'll spend days trying to figure out which college is nicknamed UN.)

Nancy's so dense that she doesn't notice her audience isn't exactly spellbound. She launches into a discussion on beauty tips, assuming you can have a discussion with yourself.

"You know what's very important when you're pregnant?" she says. "Vaseline. The most important thing we can all do is put Vaseline on our abdomens. That will help get rid of stretch marks."

I look at Cheryl, who's sitting across from me. I make a face and twirl my finger close to my temple. I must be in front of some shiny, reflective surface because Nancy notices. Evidently the sign of the twirling finger has even made its way into Mississippi.

"So you think this is funny, Anne?" Nancy says. Her voice is different. It's dripping acid instead of magnolias. "So you think this is all a big joke. Everything's funny to you, isn't it?"

I freeze, of course. I always freeze when there's any kind of confrontation. I immediately want to disappear or, better yet, die. This is because I'm a complete coward, when you get right down to it. Once I read an article in a magazine about the "passive-aggressive personality." It said passive-aggressive people are sneaky. I recognized myself immediately. That's what I am: sneaky and passive-aggressive. But at least I know it. I'm very well acquainted with all my faults.

Nancy doesn't wait for me to answer, which is just as well. I'm not about to say anything.

"We're all going to leave this home in a few months," she says in a low, angry voice. "We're going to have to go back and date again and pretend that none of this ever happened. You tell me how we can do that if we look like we've had babies. You think this is funny? Well, it's not. We still have a chance now, if we take care of ourselves. If we don't then everybody's going to know about us."

All the time she's talking, I look at the floor. I'm thinking passive-aggressive thoughts. I glance at Nancy's head to see if her roots are showing. (Not yet.) I'm also pretending I'm somewhere else. Egypt, maybe. Going through life as a passive-aggressive person requires a lot of travel. I pretend I can see the Pyramids on the floor. They're dazzling.

"I agree with Anne," I hear someone say. It's Donna. I'm not sure what she's agreeing with me about, since I haven't said anything. But Donna doesn't exactly have a firm grasp on reality.

"You act like all we have to do is smear on some Vaseline and dress great and our lives are going to be just fine," Donna says. She looks angry again, the way she did after LaNelle's baby died. "Well, that's just not true. Look at all of us." She motions around the circle. We look at each other. Nine teenage girls, all getting bigger every day.

"We're never going to be the same after any of this," Donna says. "No wonder Anne thinks it's funny. But it's worse than funny. It's pathetic."

Donna sits back and looks exhausted. No wonder. I feel exhausted too. If I get within a hundred feet of an angry person, I always want to go lie down. Being around two of them is about to kill me. I wonder why Donna's so angry these days. She hasn't said anything about Dick in ages. Maybe she's finally given up. That would be better for her. But why's she getting so angry if she's better off?

I can tell that Nancy is gearing up to say something

more, but Mrs. Landing clears her throat. "I think we've said enough for today," she says. "We all have a lot to think about over the weekend. Talking about these things seems painful." I'm sure she's looking at me, but I pretend not to notice. "But I think some good can come out of it. At least we're talking to each other now."

I now have a collection of letters from my family. Three from my mother and two from my father and two from Pamela. I've stopped opening them. I have X-ray eyes. I already know what they say, so I don't need to read them. They're sitting in my nightstand drawer, and they're growing. Every week, they're growing.

I know they're expecting me to write them back. After all, they'd say, they love me. They want to know what's going on with me.

One night I decide to amuse myself. I compose a truthful letter to my family in my head. I'm going to let them know what's really going on with me.

Dear Mother, Daddy, and Pamela,

I feel like we're a million miles away from each other. That sounds melodramatic, I know. But sometimes I feel melodramatic.

I don't hate the home as much as I did at first. I have some friends here, kind of. Last week a baby died. I'm still confused about why this bothers me so much. After all, I don't want the baby I'm carrying and I've sometimes wished it would die too.

At first I couldn't understand how some of the girls here

cared about their babies. It made me feel like something was wrong with me, since I couldn't. But recently I've been thinking a little about the baby I'm carrying and wondering about it. That makes me feel even worse and it scares me. Can you understand that? I was a lot better off when I hated it or when I didn't feel anything at all.

I feel so lonely most of the time, and so sad. You told me to think long and hard about myself and what I've done wrong and how I've hurt all of you. I know I'm supposed to say again and again how sorry I am. The fact is, you wouldn't believe how sorry I am. I'm the sorriest person on earth.

Your daughter,
Anne

After that I sit down and write the letter I'll send. I tell my family about the weather here, which is getting cooler finally, and how the food isn't too bad. I say I miss them, and I thank them for writing me so often. It means a lot to me, I say.

The Fifth Week
September 17-23

Well, here's another example of how I'm a weak person. It's Sunday, and I'm going to the movies with everyone else.

I told myself over and over that I'd never stoop this low. There was no way I was going to get on that bus with a bunch of other pregnant girls and make a spectacle of myself. But here I am, lining up with everyone else.

It's the first time I've left the home in a month, and it makes me nervous to be going somewhere. That's part of my passive-aggressive personality and being a coward and very weak and all that. Sometimes I think I should work on a new personality.

I feel strange when I get to the basket of cheap "wedding" rings right by the outside door. We all stop and put one on before we go outside. I stretch out my left hand

44

and watch the ring glint in the sunlight. It looks weird on my hand.

Mrs. Landing gets some private Methodist school to donate its bus every Sunday for these outings. Once I get inside the bus, I suspect they give us their oldest, crummiest vehicle instead of taking it straight to the junkyard, where it belongs. The seats are torn and the whole thing smells like a livestock arena. Some of us try to lower the windows so it will smell better, but most of them are stuck and won't open.

The school also donates a bus driver, who's in worse shape than the bus. He looks like a wrinkled, two-hundred-year-old mole that lost all its fur. He can barely see over the top of the steering wheel, but I'm not sure that matters, since he seems pretty blind anyway. I hope he'll wait to die of old age until we get back to the home.

The bus is big enough that we can spread out and get our own seats. I sit midway down the aisle, and Donna is in the seat in front of me. Her baby's due any day now, and her ankles are swollen and she looks as if she's going to burst. She keeps pushing her hair back from her forehead and fanning herself with a church bulletin she found on the floor. Her face looks plump and sweaty.

In the past two or three days Donna's started to go crazy again. She's been talking more and more about Dick, and her voice sounds panicked. "He'd better hurry," she said one night last week. "We don't have much time left if we're going to get married before the baby gets here."

When Donna said that, Nancy stared at her like she was completely nuts. It kills me to agree with Nancy on anything, but I have to admit she may be right for once. Donna's coming unglued.

I read *A Streetcar Named Desire* last year because our school district banned it and I wanted to stick up for the Constitution. The point is, Donna reminds me of Blanche DuBois, and I wonder if they make straitjackets that fit pregnant girls. All I know is, I don't want to be around when Donna goes into labor and finally realizes Dick isn't going to make an honest woman out of her. Maybe I can arrange to be out of the country.

On the other hand, maybe Donna isn't crazy after all. She may have a hormonal problem. I've read a few articles on hormones, and they can make you crazy, especially when you're pregnant. I hope the doctors around here know about hormones.

Today, though, Donna is acting sane again. She pulls her legs up next to her enormous stomach and talks and laughs. The rest of us are all talking and laughing too, even me. For some reason we all seem younger. Most of us are teenagers, but we act older. Ever since I got pregnant, I've felt ancient. Sometimes I can't believe I'm only seventeen. I spend lots of time feeling like I'm a hundred and seventeen. It's strange, but nice, to feel young again for a little while.

It's still hot this time of year. But once we start moving, the wind streams through the windows we managed to open, and it feels cooler. We bounce along the road, and I look out the window. I've only been here once before, when my parents brought me to the home. Nothing looks familiar. It's a flat, open prairie, with a few trees along the side of the road. You can go for miles and miles without seeing anything different.

As we get closer to town we pass by some scattered houses and businesses. Everything is pretty ramshackle. There are a few more trees on the edge of town—but it isn't much of a town. I see churches, a school, a coffee shop, a couple of clothes stores, and an old courthouse. There's a Main Street, of course, with stores and parked cars and a few people on the sidewalks. It looks dusty and run down. The movie house is kind of pretty, though. It's squat and ornate, like a well-dressed fat woman plunked down on Main Street.

The driver manages to pull the bus into a parking lot without hitting anything, which is a miracle. After we stop, it takes him about five minutes to figure out which lever opens the door. I hope he isn't going inside with us. A movie with any excitement will finish him off.

We all climb down, slowly and carefully, and walk across the gravel to the movie theater. Inside, the lobby's cold and dark, the way it always is in theaters, and it smells like fresh popcorn. I see a few people look at us when we come in, but I try not to let it bother me. No one knows me here, I remind myself. For all they know, I'm from Poland or Tibet. I try to look as foreign as possible. If anyone says anything, I'll pretend I can't speak English.

I know it's silly, but the truth is, I feel happy to be out and going somewhere. I wait in line and get a jumbo buttered popcorn and a Coke and follow the others down the aisle.

It turns out they're showing an old James Bond movie that I saw a couple of years ago. The projector is jittery, but I don't care. I'm madly in love with Sean Connery. I love the action and the scenery and the romance and I even love the bad jokes. I sit with my tub of buttered popcorn between my knees and lean back in the plush velvet seat and relax. From time to time, I try to recall if Sean's married. I'm not sure.

After a while I forget where I am and who I am. I'm part of the movie and I'm being swept away. It's wonderful.

When the credits finally run at the end, I realize this is the closest I've been to being happy since I found out I was pregnant. I've forgotten what it's like not to feel bad all the time. I wish the movie could go on and on. I wish it were a double feature. I don't want to leave. I don't want to go back. I want to stay here forever.

But everyone else is leaving. I file up the aisle, walking slowly and carefully. I'm still not used to how different my body is these days. I feel like part of it has gone on without me. I wasn't that graceful to begin with, and I feel even more awkward now. I can't imagine how Donna manages to stand up or get in and out of chairs. I hope I won't be that big when I'm nine months pregnant.

I join the other girls in the lobby, where they're all talking about the movie. They're all in love with Sean Connery too.

"It's his eyebrows," Cheryl says dreamily.

"No, it's deeper than that," Nancy says in a low voice, and we all giggle. I look around the lobby. There are a few curious glances at us, but it's not that bad. It isn't nearly as bad as I thought it would be.

We walk outside into the hot afternoon. We're all blinking and squinting in the bright sunlight as we make our way to the parking lot.

A group of teenage boys stands nearby, leaning against a brick wall. They're farm boys, I guess, with hats sloping down over their foreheads and stubby cigarettes hanging out of their mouths. They're talking and laughing in that way groups of boys always seem to, speaking in low voices and trying to act cool.

They fall silent the minute they see us. I don't look at them, but I can tell they're staring at us. It reminds me of how we look. For a little while I almost forgot. We're seven teenage girls, about the same age they are. We have fake wedding rings and oversize stomachs, and we're all moving slowly and awkwardly toward the bus. Our footsteps crunch loudly in the gravel as we move past them.

"Hey, there!" one of them calls out.

We keep walking, with our heads averted. I start to get a sick feeling in my stomach.

"Hey, there!" he repeats, even louder. "Ain't none of you girls gonna say hi? You too good for us or something?" Around him his friends hoot and whistle and laugh.

We're moving faster now. I want to get away and hide. I want to run.

One by one we climb onto the bus. They watch that too and yell and laugh some more. I can feel my cheeks flaming. I look around, and all the other girls' faces are flushed red too. None of us say anything. We don't even look each other in the eye.

We sit down and stare straight ahead. The bus driver starts the engine. He hasn't noticed anything.

It's quiet on the ride back to the home. I sit and think how stupid I've been to feel happy for a little while. Again and again I see the group of us and how we must have looked to those boys. How ridiculous we must have looked, and how sad.

I can't sleep at all that night after we get back to the home. I feel like I have another movie going on in my head. I can't forget those boys and the way they stared at us and how they yelled and what they must have thought. They looked at us in a way that makes me think they know all about us.

In high school there were always a few girls you heard about. They were usually from poor families and they wore too much makeup and ratted and dyed their hair and wore dresses that were too tight or too short or too low-cut. Sometimes you saw their names on the walls of the girls' rest room. Things like, "Barbara Davis is a whore." Sometimes whoever wrote it couldn't spell *whore* right, and someone else came along and corrected it by adding a *w*. I always wondered if Barbara Davis corrected the spelling herself. She might have been particular about that word.

Anyway, you knew those girls were loose and they "did it," and you watched the guys look at them and talk to them in a different way. You knew those girls were cheap and pathetic and sad. They didn't have anything to do with me or most of the girls I knew. We might as well have been from different planets. I was a good girl, a good student, from a good family. I'd never been popular, to put it mildly, but I was one of the "nice" girls. I knew that. Everyone knew it.

But yesterday those boys looked at us the way the boys in my high school always looked at girls like Barbara Davis. I can't believe that happened to me.

I try to get angry, the way I usually do when something upsets me. But I can't. I know those boys are right. They looked at us and they knew all about us. It's all about sex and how we got caught, but it's more than that. It's like they looked inside us and realized how horrified and dirty we feel. That's the awful part.

It makes me think of the three or four girls I knew in Dallas who got pregnant at my high school. First you started to hear rumors about a girl. Someone told you that she was "definitely p.g." Everyone knew it. You watched her closely to see if her stomach stuck out, but you couldn't tell for sure. I couldn't, at least. But then after a few weeks she disappeared. She left school, and you heard she'd gone to live with an aunt or a grandmother. But everyone knew the truth. Everyone nudged each other and winked. Even the teachers and parents talked about it. The rumors kept on flying around until everyone got bored and forgot about it.

Sometimes everyone knew who the father was. Sometimes they guessed. There was always an air of excitement around him. It made him seem older and a little dangerous, but not in a bad way.

I knew one of those girls. Her name was Jill Evans, and she was two years ahead of me in school. She had dark hair and she was always in a hurry, dashing around all the time. She was secretary of the National Honor Society, so I knew she must have been smart. She seemed nice, too. She spoke to people in the halls even when she didn't know them. Her locker was close to mine, and she usually smiled at me and said hello. That was a nice thing for an upperclassman to do.

I knew Jill was going steady with some guy. His name was Alan Everett, and he was in the Honor Society too. I didn't know him, but I knew what he looked like. He was tall and he wore glasses and looked very serious. He was supposed to be one of the smartest students in the whole school.

There weren't any rumors about Jill and Alan. They weren't the kind of people you'd ever hear rumors about. They were too smart and upstanding or something. But all of a sudden Jill dropped out of school and disappeared. Just like that, with no warning. People said things like how they couldn't believe it. Jill Evans! She always looked so innocent and nice. It was hard to believe and it was shocking, everyone said. But you could tell people were enjoying it, too.

Later I heard that Jill begged Alan to marry her, and he refused. He planned to go to MIT and he had his future to think about. I don't know if that was true or not. That was just what I heard.

Every time I saw Alan in the hall or outside the school, he seemed okay. He looked the same, like nothing had happened. He was salutatorian of his class that year, and he got a National Merit Scholarship to MIT. His future hadn't suffered much.

When all of this was going on, I thought about it for a while and then forgot about it. It didn't have anything to do with me. I hardly knew Jill. It was too bad, but it didn't affect me that much. Jill never came back to school, and no one seemed to know where she'd gone.

Then I saw her last Christmas. I'm almost positive it was her. I was at a shopping mall with my mother and Pamela, and it was crowded and noisy. People were loaded down with packages, and they kept bumping into each other. We stopped to listen to a junior high choir that was singing in front of one of the fountains. They were belting out something like "Deck the Halls," and two of the kids were clanging bells as hard as they could. They were a pretty bad choir, but lots of their parents were gathered around, listening and taking pictures.

When one of the flashbulbs popped, I looked over and saw Jill. She was standing only two people away from me. She was taller and thinner than she used to be, and she had her coat wrapped around her, even though it was hot in the mall. Then she looked at me and our eyes held for just a second before we both looked away. The next time I glanced over there, she was gone.

At first I wondered if that had really been her. That

was a dumb thing to wonder. Of course it was her. I knew that all along. I just didn't want to admit it. I told myself it had been someone who looked like Jill. That's why I hadn't smiled or spoken to her. I wasn't sure who she was.

It made me sad every time I thought about seeing her. I don't know why. Maybe I was sad because she was a nice person and then everyone talked about her and I talked too. But I felt even worse because I could have said something to her that day at the mall, or I could have waved at her or something, anything. But I didn't. I hadn't done anything.

I never told anybody I'd seen Jill. But I wondered about her sometimes. I wondered if she'd gone back to school somewhere else, and if she was happy again. She hadn't looked happy when I saw her.

I know this sounds stupid, but I always thought that once people had sex, they knew something I didn't. It was like the world was divided up between virgins and nonvirgins. I thought about that the minute I saw Jill at the mall. She looked different. She looked even more serious and mysterious.

Now it's almost a year later, and everything has changed for me. I wonder what people are saying about me these days, if they're talking about me the way they talked about Jill. Will they look at me and think I'm different, that I know something they don't? That's something I try not to think about. It's enough for me to try to get through these few months without thinking about anything else. I don't want to think about what people are saying about me now, or what they'll say when I go back to school next semester. It's bad enough being here without having to think about the future, too.

The funny thing about being here at the home is that it makes me feel safe. I don't feel happy and I'm not that close to the other girls who are here, but I do feel safe. I can stay here and pretend. I can pretend I don't have any kind of future. I can pretend there isn't another world out there where people will talk about me or laugh about me or look at me like I'm dirt. I can pretend I'm not going back to a place where people may see me someday and look the other way—the way I had with Jill.

Talk about timing. Wednesday, Donna gets a letter from a "friend." The letter is mostly devoted to telling her that Dick eloped with someone named Bette. The "friend" thinks Donna should know. What a creep.

Donna spends the morning in her room. She has the curtains drawn and it's almost dark inside. You have to get close to her bed before you can see her, lying there and crying. What's awful is how quietly she cries. Tears stream down her face, but she hardly makes a sound. It isn't at all what I expected. I expected Donna would have a big breakdown and then she'd throw herself out the window. Since this place has only one floor, it probably wouldn't be too bad. She might have ruined the flower beds, though.

But that isn't happening. Donna doesn't even go near the window. She doesn't move from her bed.

Every few minutes one of us looks in on her. Sometimes we try to say something comforting. Things like, "Well, you're better off knowing what kind of guy Dick is. He's a jerk. He would have made a horrible husband." (To be honest, I'm the one who said that, and then I felt like a dope. But what else could I say? Nothing would help. Donna doesn't seem to hear us anyway.)

By noon everything changes. Donna goes into labor, just like that. I know she's due to have her baby, but I still think the labor is all Dick's fault.

Cheryl says Donna's in "hard" labor. I don't know what that means, but it sounds bad. She's having contractions every ten minutes or so. When one comes, she grabs her stomach and lies still. The weird thing is, she actually looks better now that she's in labor. At least she's making a few noises, and she isn't crying anymore.

Cheryl and I take turns staying with her. We turn on the bedside lamp, and we sit on the empty bed next to her. Nancy comes in to help too. It must be a big struggle for her to drag herself away from the mirror. We bring Donna ice water to drink and washcloths to wipe her face. Her brown hair is matted down on her forehead in a short, damp line.

Sometimes she thanks us for helping her. Other times you can see that she's concentrating so much on the pain that she doesn't know we're here. She grits her teeth and stares up at the ceiling. Her eyes look blank.

After a couple of hours her contractions get worse. "Go tell Mrs. Landing Donna needs to go to the hospital," Cheryl says. She's been acting bossy ever since she figured out she knows a lot more about labor than I do. I don't care, though. I'm pretty sure I don't want to learn much more about labor. Let everyone else be an expert about it. That's fine with me.

I have to wait around Mrs. Landing's office till she finally gets off the phone. By the time she and I get back to Donna's room, three or four girls are standing outside her door. Cheryl comes out of the room when Mrs. Landing goes in.

"Donna just had a couple of bad contractions," Cheryl says excitedly. "You should have heard her. She started cussing up a storm. First she said she wasn't going to name the baby Dick Jr., the way she'd planned. She said she'd always hated the name Dick anyway. Then she starting swearing about Dick and Bette. She said she hoped they'd go driving in Dick's precious blue-and-white '57 Chevy and get hit by a train. She said that would serve Dick right. He'd always been a bad driver anyway, and his car was a piece of junk and Bette was a two-bit slut. She said she wouldn't go to their funeral if everyone begged her."

Cheryl looks quite pleased about all of this. "Nancy and I thought that all that swearing and screaming was a good sign," she says. "We almost started applauding."

A few minutes later Mrs. Landing helps Donna walk between her contractions. Cheryl gets on Donna's other side, and they lead her slowly out to a car. When a contraction comes, they stop and wait till it's over. It takes them almost ten minutes to get her into the car.

A few of us stand outside on the porch and watch them leave. The heat has finally broken, and it's cloudy and raining. The cool, damp air feels good since we've been inside Donna's room for so long. We wave at the car as it drives away, splashing water and mud on the side of the road.

Back inside, our moods are lightened for some reason. Cheryl is trying to straighten Donna's room. I help her a little and look around for Donna's guitar. I still haven't seen it. Maybe she packed it to take to the hospital.

After dinner we hear that Donna had a healthy, seven-pound baby girl. It strikes us as funny. So much for Dick Jr., we all say.

The Sixth Week
September 24-30

One night I dream I'm making love. I've never dreamed that before.

I'm not sure who the guy is. I look at him, but I can't quite see his face. I know that he loves me, though.

In the dream he lies on top of me and we move together. I feel like I'm floating up into the sky. There are stars bursting inside me, and they keep bursting again and again. He and I look at each other, and he tells me he loves me and he keeps moving inside me. It feels wonderful.

When I wake up, I lie in bed and stretch luxuriously. I don't want to get up. I feel too good, lying there. I feel beautiful and loved and warm all over.

I stretch some more and lie there for a few minutes, and slowly the warmth leaves me. I begin to feel sadder and sadder. For two months I made love with Jake, and he never looked me in the face and he never loved me. I wanted him to make me feel beautiful and loved. I wanted him to feel the same way about me that I felt about him. But he never had. I knew that, even then.

For two months we made love, if you want to call it that. But I never got any pleasure from it. It never made me feel warm and good, the way the dream had. It always left me cold and sad and alone, the way I feel now.

I haven't thought about Jake in weeks. I worked hard at trying not to think about him. But ever since I had that dream, he's all I can think about. I see his face every time I close my eyes. It makes me wonder that if I think about him all the time for several days, he'll disappear and I'll never think about him again.

I'm not like the others. I'm not like Donna or LaNelle. I can't go to the meetings and talk about him and how I feel about him. I wish I could, but I can't. I'd like to talk about him for hours and hours, and cry and scream and drain him from my life and my mind. But I can't. I've never even spoken his name here. I could move my lips, but no sound would come out.

If I could talk about it, this is the story I'd tell.

I noticed Jake the first time last January. I can still feel how that day was. It was the kind of day when the rain blurred the windows at school, and the wind blew, and the tress were stark and bare.

I was in the library after school, and I looked up from my book and saw him watching me. He was thin and good looking, with straight dark hair that sometimes fell into his face. I know I must have blushed, and I looked back at my book right away. I was like that with boys, especially nice-looking ones. I was a junior in high school and I'd had about three dates in my life, and they'd all been disasters. I would have thought about joining a convent, but my family was Presbyterian.

Pamela was the popular one in the family. Boys had been calling her since she was in sixth grade, and she went out on dates every weekend. I hated having a sister who was popular. I especially hated having a younger sister who was popular. Every Friday and Saturday night I'd go to my room and try to read so I couldn't hear the doorbell ring. I didn't want to see Pamela parading out with her date. If I was feeling bad, I used to imagine she'd trip going down the stairs and break her leg or collarbone.

My parents loved it, of course. They loved having at least one daughter who was pretty and popular and extroverted. They were thrilled when Pamela was elected freshman class queen last September. Boy, did I hate that week. That's when I began to think more and more seriously about the convent idea. I knew I'd have to become a Catholic, but it might be worth it in the long run. No one expected nuns to have dates on the weekend. None of their sisters ever went out on dates, either.

The funny thing was, I knew I wasn't unpopular because I was ugly or anything. I looked okay, and sometimes people said I was pretty. I never felt pretty, though. All I ever felt was shy.

The more I wanted to talk to a boy, the more I

couldn't say anything. When I talked, my voice would get high-pitched and shaky and I'd turn red and say something stupid. After a while I gave up trying. If I didn't try at all, I thought, then I wouldn't feel like a fool.

I told myself I was the intellectual type. I'd graduate from high school and go on to college and work hard, and I'd have a wonderful, glamorous career somewhere far away. And no one would ever know that I never dated in high school and I never went to the prom. Years later it wouldn't matter.

By then Pamela would be living in a trailer park somewhere, and she'd be fat. She'd have seven children and an unemployed husband with a drinking problem and a part-time job in a bowling alley picking up pins. It would be very sad.

As for me, I'd be living in a Manhattan high-rise. I'd have a fabulous career and an adoring husband who loved me for myself and my quietly sparkling personality. I would also have grown very big breasts. I'd look back at myself in high school and laugh softly. If I'd only known then what a great life I'd eventually have!

So that was my life and those were my dreams. I know they sound demented, but if I tried hard enough, I believed them and they kept me going. I had some kind of stupid faith that someday my life would be good and I'd be happy. It makes me sad now to think of how dumb I was then, and how everything has turned out to be so different.

· · ·

Once I start thinking about Jake, I can't stop. That's because I'm a very obsessive person. I asked my mother one time if I could see a psychiatrist because I had lots of personality problems, like being obsessive. My mother seemed to think that was funny.

"You don't even know what personality problems are, Anne," she said. She started laughing, and she sounded strange. "You don't even know what problems are," she told me. "You'll find out when you grow up."

So I've never seen a psychiatrist and I'm still very obsessive and all those other things I've mentioned. That's why I keep thinking about Jake. I can't help it. It's my personality. But anyway, here's how it all happened.

It started about a month after I'd noticed Jake in the library. Pamela's boyfriend was out of town for some reason, maybe for some kind of remedial reading classes for football players, and Pamela wanted to go to a dance at the youth center. Naturally she couldn't go alone. Pamela never did anything alone. She even left the door open when she went to the bathroom. I always shut my eyes when I had to walk past her. It never occurred to her that other people might think it was gross to see her going to the bathroom. Lots of things never occurred to Pamela. She was an exhibitionist, when you got right down to it.

My mother started pushing me to go to the dance with Pamela. "You never know who you'll meet there," she said, and winked at me. My mother was like that. She was always telling me that my high school days were the best of my life. Boy, did I find that a depressing thought. She also told me other things she thought were helpful, such as asking boys about themselves and listening to them carefully so I could ask them more questions and they could talk more about themselves. A few times she pointed out that boys didn't like girls who acted too smart. Once I said I guessed that's why Pamela was so popular, and my mother slapped me in the face. It was the only time she ever slapped me. We both looked surprised, but she never apologized for it.

But I went to the dance that night because I could tell my mother wasn't going to leave me alone. She was in one of her bad moods, and it was easier for me to go.

The minute I got to the dance, I hated it. It was dark and crowded, and the music was loud and not very good. The lead guitarist talked in between songs, and I noticed he was trying to sound like he was English. Everybody wanted to sound English then, especially if they were in a band. This guy was trying hard, but you could tell he was probably from Fort Worth or somewhere even worse.

Pamela had already disappeared, of course. "You don't mind, do you, Anne?" she asked me before she rushed off to the dance floor with the first guy she made eye contact with. That had been fifteen minutes ago, and I hadn't seen her since. I stood off to the side of the room and hoped it was too dark for anybody to see me. I stared down at my Coke and watched the ice cubes bob up and down and the bubbles break.

They were playing a slow dance now, and out of the corner of my eye I could see couples intertwined on the dance floor. I didn't want to look at my watch yet, because I knew it was still early. I was never, ever going to let my mother talk me into something like this again, I decided. I planned to spend the rest of my life in my room, where no one could see me.

"Do you want to dance?" The voice was so close to me that I almost jumped. I looked up into Jake's face, and I nodded. That was all I could do. I was too surprised to say anything.

He caught my hand and pulled me onto the dance floor. The slow song was still playing. I wrapped my arms around his neck, and he put his hands on my waist and pulled me closer to him. I'd only danced like that a few times before. I closed my eyes and I couldn't see anything, and I couldn't hear the music, either. I was somewhere far away, alone with him and floating.

I'll tell you what's awful about remembering this story. Part of me returns to it and I feel like I'm there. And the other part stays here, and laughs and shakes her head. It's bad enough to have been an idiot. It's a lot worse to still be one.

You could empty out every romance novel, and that's what you would have found in my head last spring. Name a cliché and I was feeling it. My heart was bursting. The world was full and bright and exciting. Even the colors were more vivid and the music was better. I'd never been in love before, and I had no idea what it would feel like.

The dogwoods and azaleas bloomed, and I'd never

seen a more gorgeous spring in my life. I can remember lying on a blanket in the park with Jake, looking up and watching the clouds drift past like big, white ships. We talked and we laughed, and for some reason I felt comfortable with him. I could be myself. I'm not sure what we talked about. College, maybe. Or how much we hated high school. What I remember best about that day was his voice. It was husky and soft, and he spoke with a drawl. I loved his drawl, the way he'd linger on words just a little too long.

I can't explain what it was about him that made me love him. I didn't understand it myself. All I knew was he made me feel alive. When I was with him, I felt light and buoyant and joyous. I was flying.

That day at the park he rolled over and kissed me, again and again, gently and sweetly. I touched his dark hair and kissed him back, and it seemed like the most natural thing in the world.

I was happier than I'd ever been in my life. It scared me, because I knew it couldn't last. Sometimes I realized that, then I rushed past it and went on. I didn't want to think about it. Everything was a blur to me that spring except for Jake. My schoolwork, my family, even the books I'd spent most of my time with. I'd stare at the same page for hours. But I didn't care. All I cared about was Jake.

I'd always laughed at girls like Pamela who were boy crazy. And now here I was, just like them, or maybe worse.

For the first few weeks I felt beautiful every time Jake looked at me. That had never happened to me before. It was like I was a character in one of my books. I was interesting and full of life. I was someone else I'd always wanted to be.

As I said, I'd never had a boyfriend before. There were so many things I didn't understand. I had a few friends, but most of them hadn't dated any more than I had. There was no one I could talk to about Jake.

My parents never talked much to me about getting pregnant or going "too far." I was the daughter they never worried about. I was the sensible one, unlike Pamela. There was no reason to waste their time talking to the daughter who didn't date. Years ago my mother had told me the facts of life, sort of. I knew that if you wanted boys to respect you, you wouldn't go too far. I knew that girls were the ones who had to say no and set limits.

But I never realized how good all of this would feel and how impossible it would be to stop. The first time Jake tried to unbutton my blouse, I wouldn't let him. I pushed his hand away and kissed him. The trouble was, I didn't want to stop him. Everywhere he touched me it felt wonderful, like some sort of soft, hot glow.

After a few weeks I didn't stop him. I didn't care. When he stroked my breasts and when he slid his finger inside my panties, I didn't want him to quit. I wanted to stay where we were forever. It felt wonderful. I'd never realized how wonderful it would feel.

I'd like to stop at this point. I wish I had, but I didn't. I couldn't.

Everything was different once we started to have sex. All of a sudden the long hours we'd spent making out were gone. The time we spent together seemed much more rushed and frantic. We didn't go anywhere, except to a park by a lake a few miles away, where we could be by ourselves. Sometimes we'd stay in the car and sometimes we'd get a blanket and lie on the grass. And then we'd have sex, and it would all be over in just a few minutes. It was all so hurried and almost rough, and it made me think that having sex had taken me to a completely different world.

Most of the time Jake only acted tender and loving after he'd come. That was the only time he seemed to notice me. Sometimes when he was thrusting and pushing in me, I felt like I could have been anyone. It didn't matter who I was. It didn't matter, either, that I didn't enjoy it. He never noticed, one way or the other. Sometimes I noticed, but I didn't care. I just wanted to make him happy.

It was strange to me how easy it was to have sex, but how hard it was to talk about it. We never talked about it. After we started having sex, we never talked much about anything. We never looked each other in the face. We were just in the car or out of it, having sex. And for a few minutes Jake would be with me and then he wouldn't be. The more we had sex, the further apart we seemed.

I usually felt like crying after it was over. I wasn't sure

why. It just made me sad. We'd finish and I'd sometimes have tears rolling down my cheeks, and Jake would hold me. But that never made me feel much better.

I said I knew about the facts of life, and I did. I knew there were things you could do, like use douches. Once when I was in junior high, I'd seen a rubber on the ground. Everyone had walked around it and pointed and laughed. I couldn't imagine using something like that. I knew you could buy them at the drugstore, but I couldn't imagine buying one myself or asking Jake to buy one. It wouldn't have seemed right.

I didn't know what I was doing, and I didn't know how to stop. At night I'd have dreams that I was in a car that was out of control, and I couldn't find the brake. It didn't take a genius to figure out dreams like that. I knew my life was out of control, but there was nothing I could do about it.

I can't bear to think about this any longer. I know that maybe I should push myself and think about it more and get it over with. But I can't do it. It makes me too sad. Maybe if I wait to think about this till later, it won't hurt as much. Maybe I'll forget all about it.

So I'm trying to think about other things. I'm trying very hard. Fortunately there's a lot going on around here.

It's Monday, and another new girl's arrived. Her name is Rachel and I wish someone would slip her a Valium. I know pretty much about Valium because that's what my mother takes all the time. It always seems to calm her down and make her nicer. It makes her sleep a lot, too. Sometimes she sleeps for a whole day.

You can tell that Rachel isn't taking Valium, even though she needs it. She has way too much energy. I've read that it can be bad for girls to have too much energy. It makes you self-destructive or something.

Even Rachel's hair seems nervous. It's wild looking, curly and dark and long. Her dress looks like a muumuu, but I think it's a hippie dress. She's from California. I know this because she's already told us at least twenty times. "The Bay Area," she says, and I can tell we're supposed to be impressed. Rachel must not realize there's more than one bay in the world, because she looks shocked when someone asks her which bay she's talking about. She looks as if that's the most ignorant question she's ever heard.

After five minutes I can tell Rachel thinks we're all a bunch of illiterate morons. She refers to this area as "the sticks." Boy, does that irritate me. I don't like it here either, but it makes me mad to hear Rachel complain about it. She even calls Texas a "hick state." I can't believe that. I'm thinking about reporting her to the police. She could probably go to prison for saying something like that around here.

The only thing that doesn't irritate me about Rachel is seeing how she and Nancy immediately hate each other. I can tell Nancy's dying to offer her some kind of beauty tips. I half expect her to suggest that Rachel set her hair on orange-juice cans so it won't be so frizzy and weird. But for once Nancy doesn't say much. That's the only good thing I can say about the meeting.

Most of the time Rachel's jumping in to offer everybody advice. She must think she's some kind of missionary who's been sent here to teach the Stone Age natives.

"I'm planning to keep my baby," she says. She's told us that at least four times. I guess she thinks she has to repeat herself a lot since we're all so stupid. "I'll only be here for three months," she says, "and then I'm going back to California. I'm going to be a single mother and bring up my own child."

She looks at all of us sadly. "I know the rest of you aren't as fortunate as I am. You can do things like that in California because it's such a progressive state. I know the rest of the country isn't like that. But you all need to think about keeping your babies. It's unnatural to give them up."

She goes on talking like that, in a very pushy way. I start wondering about the odds of getting so many crazy people in an unwed mothers' home. I thought we reached our quota with Donna—and now here's Rachel, wild eyed and clearly a fruitcake. If she's going to keep her baby, why didn't she just stay in California?

Nancy asks her that finally. "If California's so great, why're you here?" she says.

Rachel looks furious. I wonder if she's going to pull a knife and slit Nancy's throat. That would solve lots of problems. But she doesn't. She just looks at Nancy like she's some kind of bug that needs to be stepped on and says, "Well, obviously it's not that simple."

After the meeting's over I hear Nancy talking loudly about Rachel. She says she suspects Rachel is Jewish.

"She would have been much more comfortable staying in California," Nancy is telling someone. "There are lots of Jews in California. Lots of hippies, too."

Nancy says her mother will die if she realizes she's sent her only child off to a home where she has to hang around with a Jewish hippie. "I just hope my mother never finds out," she says.

As the week goes on, there's practically open warfare between Rachel and Nancy. It's very satisfying. I don't take sides since I don't like either one of them.

Rachel keeps on lecturing us. She's always blabbing about California and how it's so enlightened and how people there are so much more politically aware.

"I once saw Bob Dylan in a coffee shop in San Francisco," she says. "Everyone there was so cool that they pretended they didn't even know who he was."

No one says anything. So she clears her throat very loudly and says, "You know, Bob Dylan is a very famous singer."

"We know who he is," Nancy says. "We're just not interested in him. He whines when he sings and his hair looks like a bad mop. Somebody should straighten his hair for him." She stares at Rachel's hair when she says that.

After that things get a little ugly, and Mrs. Landing

looks perturbed. I can tell she thinks we aren't talking about anything important. She's right, but I don't care. Listening to Nancy and Rachel argue is like being at a tennis match. At least it takes my mind off lots of other things.

"It's time for us to quit," Mrs. Landing says a few minutes later. "Remember, we won't be meeting on Monday. You're all scheduled to see the social worker. Maybe a day off will give you all time to think."

The Seventh Week
October 1-7

I've been thinking about the fact that I'm kind of a negative person. Sometimes that bothers me, and I decide that I need to be more positive.

My mother always told me I was too negative. She had lots of positive sayings taped to the kitchen cabinet doors. Things like, "Your attitude makes all the difference!" and "A smile will protect you!" My mother always said she was a very positive, optimistic person, but she never seemed very happy to me. Maybe I was wrong, though.

But anyway, I've decided that I need to be more positive. I was honestly trying when I went to meet that social worker. It wasn't my fault that I hated her on sight.

She was in the same room that Dr. Blanchard uses to examine us in on Saturdays. It's a spare office that's down the hall from our rooms. The office is about as luxurious as all the other rooms in this place. It has a fake-wood desk and a braided rug that must have been feeding the local moths for years. Someone closed the venetian blinds at the windows, and they look like long, yellow teeth with slits of light shining through them.

The social worker is shorter than I am and probably weighs about 50 pounds more, even though she isn't pregnant. She has thin, curly brown hair, and she wears glasses that make her eyes look too big. She reached out to shake my hand when I came in, and she said, "Hello, Anne. I'm Mrs. Harris, and I'm going to be your social worker."

That gets us off to a bad start. I hate it when adults introduce themselves that way, like "Mrs." or "Mr." is their first name. She must think I can't read her name tag, which says "Shelia Harris, M.S.W." That bothers me too. How can I trust someone who can't even spell "Sheila" right? Also, I know what "M.S.W." stands for, and it isn't exactly "Ph.D."

Mrs. Harris must have taken too many of those "How to Meet People and Force Them to Like You" seminars. She stares me in the face, and when she shakes my hand, I can almost hear my knuckles pop. Maybe she thinks a firm handshake means you have to break the other person's fingers. She's one of those people who like to stand too close to you, which she shouldn't do, since her breath is pretty bad.

But I remember how I'm going to be a more positive

person, so I look at Mrs. Harris to find something to like about her. Finally I decide that her dress isn't too bad if you like loud primary colors, which I don't.

Mrs. Harris obviously thinks we've gotten off to a great start, what with the firm handshake and eye contact. So she sits down for a few minutes and stares at my file. She's a very slow reader.

I sit down too and start biting my fingernails. That's my newest bad habit. I wonder what my father will say about it. He hates people who do things like bite their nails or smoke. He says it shows they don't have any self-control and that it's bad form to let other people know how nervous you are.

"You're from Dallas, I see," Mrs. Harris says. I agree I am. "And your father's a lawyer and your mother's a housewife . . . and you have a younger sister named Pamela." Her voice trails off as she reads more. "Very good grades, I see," she murmurs. "National Honor Society . . . Spanish club . . . very high test scores."

She breaks off and looks at me. It's one of those sincere looks that I've never trusted. "Anne," she says, "I'm here to help you. I'm someone you can come to anytime you feel you have a problem. I want you to know I don't judge you like the rest of the world does. I'm here to be your friend, and I want you to feel free to talk to me about anything.

"I should tell you," she goes on, "that I think you're doing something very brave and wonderful. It would have been easy for you to have an abortion. Lots of girls do that. They go to Mexico, and they just get rid of the baby. But you didn't. You chose to have this baby and to give it up so it can have a better life. I want you to know that you've made the right decision—and that I admire you tremendously for that decision."

She smiles at me, and I know I'm supposed to be grateful. She hasn't known me for ten minutes, and she's already decided I'm a wonderful person she can respect and admire. That isn't any worse than my own snap judgment that she's an insincere creep who knows as much about me as I know about quantum physics.

I don't want Mrs. Harris's admiration or friendship. I stare at the moth-eaten rug and brood and sulk. I think about Delia, one of the maids we used to have at our house in Dallas. When Delia got pissed off at my mother, which happened every two or three minutes, she'd go around muttering, "You can stick it where the sun don't shine, lady." My mother always pretended not to hear her say that, since she didn't want to clean the house herself. I've always loved that saying, even if I've never had the nerve to use it. That's what I want to tell Mrs. Harris to do with all her syrupy goodwill. Stick it where the sun don't shine, lady.

If I had any guts, I'd start screaming and crying and making up lots of big lies to tell Mrs. Harris. I'd tell her how I want to keep my baby and run off to the drug commune where my boyfriend is. Sure, he's a convicted felon, but he hasn't violated parole in six months and I'm very proud of him. People don't give him a chance when they hear his nickname is Killer. Killer loves me so much he's going to get the tattoo with his third wife's name taken off his left buttock. Isn't that beautiful? Does Mrs. Harris realize how painful it is to have a tattoo taken off your rear end? That shows Killer truly loves me, doesn't she think? Also, doesn't he sound like he'll be a great father?

I keep adding to the story and changing it in my head. Maybe I'll say the father of the baby is a Catholic priest named Father Bud. Or that I had sex with my family's Irish setter. Does that mean the baby won't be an American?

I don't say any of this, of course. I start to realize that being around Mrs. Harris is making me crazy and possibly perverted, so I need to get away from her as soon as possible.

"Would you like to tell me about the father of your child, Anne?" she asks.

"No," I say. You could hold a gun to my head and I wouldn't discuss anything personal with this woman. Let her think she knows all about me. She doesn't know anything about me or my life. All I want is to get out of her office and never see her again.

Mrs. Harris says she understands that it may be "too early" for me to talk to her and to trust her. "But that will come in time," she says.

She gives me one of those big, sympathetic social worker smiles, and I feel like I'm drowning in molasses. It's only ten o'clock in the morning, and my resolutions

about being more positive have already gone straight
to hell.

Donna comes back to get her clothes on Wednesday. I
almost don't recognize her. Her short brown hair is styl-
ishly combed, and she's wearing makeup and a pink-
and-white baby-doll dress. She looks like a normal
person, and for a few minutes I can't believe that she
used to live here. I wonder if everything changes the
minute you have your baby. Do you have it and get
dressed and comb your hair and walk off and everything
is normal?

Maybe Donna isn't crazy any longer either. I look at
her face, and she doesn't seem crazy. She just looks tired.
She's still trying to smile and act cheerful, the way she
did when she lived here.

Cheryl and I go in Donna's room to talk to her while
she packs. While Donna was in the hospital, Rachel
moved into the room. She has a stereo, and she plays Bob
Dylan albums on it twenty-four hours a day. "Don't
Think Twice, It's All Right" is her favorite song, so she
plays it practically every ten minutes. She says it's "very
poetic." She actually uses that word, *poetic.*

Rachel decorated the room in a very tacky way. She
put up lots of big, ugly posters on the wall. One is a
big photograph of President Johnson, and it says WAR
CRIMINAL under it.

Rachel hates LBJ. "I strongly suspect that he was
involved in John F. Kennedy's assassination," she an-

nounced one day. She was practically whispering, as if she was telling some big secret the FBI would be interested in hearing. "Think about it. Kennedy was killed in Johnson's home state. Lots of people—lots of very brilliant people—think there's a connection there."

When she heard I'm from Dallas, Rachel acted like I was personally responsible for the assassination too. She said most people blame Dallas for Kennedy's death. "I was scared to death when my plane had to land at the Dallas airport on the way here," she said. "I think it's a very dangerous thing for liberals to go to Dallas."

Not dangerous enough, I kept thinking. As usual, I didn't say anything. I tried to give Rachel the evil eye when she wasn't looking.

Rachel also goes out of her way to make snide comments about Lady Bird Johnson. "If she really wants to beautify the country," she said several million times, "she should start with her own two daughters."

Actually I think Lady Bird should start right in this room. Rachel has wretched taste. She has lots of rock posters on the walls that she's proud of, for some reason. Most of them show vile-looking band members. You could probably get a social disease just by looking at them. Maybe Rachel hasn't noticed how seedy they are. She may need glasses or a cornea transplant.

Rachel doesn't have a roommate yet, and I pity whoever moves in with her. Maybe they can get someone who doesn't speak English and won't understand anything Rachel says. That would be for the best. Either that or maybe they can move Nancy in here and she and Rachel will kill each other. I like that idea even better.

Fortunately Rachel isn't here now, so Donna can pack her clothes in peace. After a few minutes Cheryl and I can't help ourselves. We start asking her questions. I don't want to, but there are so many things I'm dying to know. How bad is labor? Did it hurt terribly? Did she see the baby? And what about Dick? Does he know about the baby?

Donna's face changes a little, getting tighter around her mouth. But she keeps on packing her clothes. She says that childbirth wasn't that bad. Sure, it hurt. But she expected that. No, she didn't see the baby. The nurses wouldn't let her.

She sits down on her bed and folds a dress. She turns it over and over, folding it again and again, until she rolls it into a ball. Then she sits there and clenches it between her hands.

"I never saw my baby," she says. "They told me I had a little girl, but I never saw her. My milk came in, and they gave me shots so it would dry up. But it didn't at first. For two days every time I heard a baby cry, my milk came in. I wondered if I was hearing my baby cry, and that's why my milk was coming in. I asked one of the nurses that once, and she said no. They'd moved my baby to another part of the hospital, and I couldn't hear her. I didn't know if that was the truth or not."

Donna's eyes fill with tears. "I never thought this would happen to me," she says. "I know it was dumb and I know all of you thought I was crazy. But all along I thought Dick would realize how much he loved me and how he couldn't live without me and the baby. That's how I got through all those months, thinking the three of us would be together. Now I'm going home alone, and I don't know how I'm going to live."

She bends her head over the wadded-up dress and starts to sob. It makes a sad, lonely sound in the room.

I think of how angry Donna was at Mrs. Landing after LaNelle's baby died, and at Nancy that day in the group meeting. I remember how she swore about Dick and Bette when she went into labor. She was angry then, too.

I wish she'd get angry again. Anything but this. But she doesn't. She lies on her bed and she sobs for a long time, and then she's quiet. Cheryl and I try to talk to her and tell her everything will be all right. "I think I need to be alone now," Donna tells us, so Cheryl and I finally leave the room because we can't think of anything else to do.

Donna leaves early on Thursday before we get up. She doesn't say good-bye to any of us. She just leaves and goes back to her hometown. It's a small town somewhere in central Texas. She'll probably run into that no-good jerk Dick one of these days.

"Maybe Donna will see Dick trying to cross the street when she's driving one day," I say to Cheryl. "And all of a sudden her gas pedal will get stuck, and she'll have to choose between hitting Dick and a group of kinder-garteners on a field trip. Naturally she'll have to run over Dick. But no jury would ever convict her, of course."

I love creating scenarios like that. They're much more satisfying than real life.

"Since Dick was broke when he died, he'll have to be buried in a paupers' field," I add. I'm not sure there are paupers' fields in Texas, but I think the general idea is quite appealing. "Only three people will come to Dick's funeral, and no one will cry. The minister will call him Rick all the way through the service, and no one will correct him."

Cheryl is laughing by this time, but I don't go on. After seeing Donna the night before, I realize it's likelier she'll get in her car and drive off a cliff by herself. She seemed resigned and horribly depressed. She probably won't run over Dick even if she gets the chance. That's too bad.

Nancy brings that up when we have our meeting. "Donna was probably a good person," she says, "but she was a fool. She trusted her boyfriend too much, and he let her down. She should have been watching out for herself all along."

I'm amazed. This is the first time Nancy's talked about anyone but herself. It's also one of the few interesting things I've ever heard her say. Maybe she's read a book. This may be an evolutionary breakthrough.

Even Mrs. Landing looks surprised. "What do you mean, Nancy?" she asks. "Are you saying that you can't trust anyone—that you're a fool to trust another person?"

"I'm saying you have to be a fool to trust a man," Nancy says. She looks mad for some reason. "You might as well throw your life away. Men want sex out of us, that's all. Once they get it, they leave and they don't give a damn about what happens to us. They'll break your heart if you let them. I've seen it happen to a lot of women. That's what happened to Donna—and maybe that's what happened to the rest of you—but it's not going to happen to me. I'm not going to let it happen."

She looks even angrier now. She's practically glaring at the rest of us, like we're her enemy.

It's funny, I think. Here's Nancy, who's seven or eight months pregnant and in an unwed mothers' home. And she's saying that she's different from Donna and everyone else who's here. I give her ten points for having a lot of nerve and minus fifty points for being an idiot. So much for her evolution.

Rachel jumps into the discussion—naturally. As usual she tries to make something political out of it. "I think what Nancy is trying to say is that women need to take control of their lives," she says. "We have to take responsibility for ourselves. That's what women's liberation is all about."

Oh, great. Women's liberation. Rachel's going to suggest we build a bonfire and burn our maternity bras. That will certainly make everything better. Maybe we can burn a man in effigy, too. That will show we're taking control of our lives.

"That's not at all what I was saying," Nancy says, sounding irritated. "This has nothing to do with women's liberation, for God's sake. I've never seen anything liberating about not shaving your underarms and trying to look as ugly as possible. What I'm saying is completely different. I'm saying we need to get what we can out of men—the same way they get what they can out of us. I want a life that's better than my mother's—and you tell me how I'm going to get that without a man."

Rachel tells Nancy she's deranged and manipulative. "All you're doing is trying to live through a man," she says.

"You've missed the point—as usual," Nancy snaps. "If you're a girl, you don't have that many choices, but you do have a few. You can control men—or you can let them control you."

Since I never say anything, I sit and listen. Rachel launches into her usual blabbing about how everything is changing. Everything is just great these days, according to her.

"Women are getting more power," she says. "But we have to work for it. We live in an evil, sexist society and we have to fight it. That's one reason why I want to keep my baby. I want to show that a woman can survive by herself."

"You're nuts," Nancy says. "You're going to end up on welfare with your bastard child. If you want to call that liberation, that's fine. It sounds like hell on wheels to me."

Rachel objects to the word *bastard*, of course. That word is further evidence of how sick our society is and how much it needs to be changed, she says.

She and Nancy talk on and on. That's all they ever do,

talk. They're both lunatics. They can talk forever, and it won't matter. It doesn't change the fact that we are all sitting here, getting bigger every day.

These days I don't recognize my own body. It's not mine any longer. It belongs to someone else. In ten weeks I'll give birth.

I wanted to think that I could walk away then and everything would be all right. Just another few weeks, I kept telling myself, and I'd be free. I could go back to my old life. I'd be thin again, and I'd wear my old clothes and I'd go back to school and continue to do well. My life would pick up and be the same, and I would have only missed a few months out of it. If I worked hard and took summer school classes, I could even go to college next year. I hoped for all of that.

Maybe I can go back and my parents will forgive me and no one will have to know that I had a baby. But sometimes I'm not sure about that. Sometimes I feel that something in me has changed forever, and my life will never be the same.

That's what happened to Donna. She had her baby, and her body looked normal now. If you didn't know her, maybe you'd think she looked all right. But I looked at her closely, and she seemed haunted somehow. As far as I could tell, she hadn't managed to walk away from anything. She'd taken it all with her.

On Saturday, Cheryl gets a letter from LaNelle, and she seems excited about it. It makes me realize that Cheryl doesn't get much mail. In fact, I can't recall if she's ever gotten a letter before. But maybe she has. Maybe she has and she doesn't talk about it, like me.

Cheryl says the letter is for all of us. Nancy comes in the room to listen to it. Then Rachel. That annoys me. Neither of them knows LaNelle. They aren't her friends. I know I'm not either, but at least I was at the home when she was. It's none of their business what LaNelle wrote. I'm sure they're here just to irritate each other.

None of that bothers Cheryl. She's still a lot nicer than I am. She and I aren't close friends these days, but we are friends, sort of. That's strange, because we don't know much about each other.

All I know about Cheryl is that she's from a small town in Oklahoma. She has three younger brothers and she likes kids a lot and she's way too religious. She didn't grow up on a farm the way I suspected, which is disappointing. "Not everybody in Oklahoma lives on a farm, Anne," is the way she put it. (At least Cheryl has a decent sense of humor. If I shared a room with someone like Harriet, who never thinks anything's funny, I'd break out in a rash and get lots of pimples. People like Harriet are very bad for my complexion.)

Rachel and Nancy make themselves right at home and sit on one of our beds, and Cheryl reads the letter to us. LaNelle says she's doing better. She has a job in a grocery store. Right now she's bagging groceries. But she hopes to become a cashier soon. She isn't going to be able to go to junior college in the spring because money's too tight at home. Maybe next fall, though.

"I visit Laurie's grave once a week, on Sundays,"

Cheryl reads. "I always bring some flowers I've picked and then I cry. Sometimes I trace the letters on her tombstone with my fingers, and I say her name out loud. What makes me sad is that no one remembers her but me. My parents never talk about her. They act like she never lived at all and she never had a name. That's why I always say her name when I'm there. I want to hear someone say it, even if it's just me."

That's the end of the letter. She signed it "Love, LaNelle," and that's it. The letter makes me feel terrible. I can see LaNelle at the cemetery, talking to her daughter's grave. I can't imagine how alone she must feel. I think about how LaNelle drove me crazy all the time she was at the home, and now I feel guilty about it. She wasn't a bad person—just an annoying one.

I've finally figured out something about LaNelle and everyone else I know at the home. Take the girls who are in the room right now. There's Cheryl, who I like, and Rachel and Nancy, who regularly drive me crazy. And LaNelle, who could come back to the home now and we still wouldn't be close friends.

But none of that matters, really. All of this goes way beyond liking or disliking. They all know what it's like to be here. They know what it's like to be pregnant and alone and scared to death.

We're all completely different, and maybe we wouldn't have picked each other as friends. But sometimes I think we understand each other better than anyone else will, ever, for the rest of our lives.

The Eighth Week
October 8-14

On Sunday my family calls me long distance. It's the first time I've talked to them since I've been here.

The three of them are on separate extensions so they can all talk to me at the same time. Pamela's the first one to get off. She says she has to study. I know what that means: she's already flunking at least one class. Probably my parents are doing something drastic like saying she can't date Bob until she learns to read.

My mother stays on the line a few minutes longer. She says she's been praying for me every day.

"Prayer makes such a big difference, Anne," she says. "I always feel so peaceful when I pray. I hope you'll start praying with me when you come home. I'd also love for you to come to church with me. There are such wonderful people in our congregation, and they'll want to welcome you back."

I hate it when my mother says things like that. I wonder if praying makes her feel more peaceful than Valium does. I also hate to hear about all those wonderful people in the congregation who want to welcome me back. They think I'm in boarding school in Switzerland, so what's the big deal?

Or maybe they know the truth. Maybe everyone knows about me and where I am. It kills me to think that, but I know it might be true. I don't want people whispering behind my back, and looking at me strangely and feeling sorry for me. I don't want them talking about who the father of my baby is. And I certainly don't want to go to church with my mother and have these people feel great about themselves because they're opening their arms to some little hard-luck sinner who's come back to the fold.

That makes me think of the Prodigal Son. I've always hated that story. Most of my life I identified with the older brother, and I always thought he got a raw deal. These days I'm more like the prodigal son himself, and I don't like that role any better. I hate the whole damn story. Come to think of it, I hate the whole damn Bible.

It doesn't seem to bother my mother that I'm not saying much. She's talking in that chirpy voice she uses when she's completely out of touch with reality. I hope she isn't heading for another breakdown. When I was twelve, she spent four weeks in an institution. She was a different person when she came back. Her eyes looked funny and dazed all the time. I wondered if my real mother was still at the institution and they'd sent someone else to our home. It was like living in a plot for *The Twilight Zone.*

But she sounds cheerful right now. "When you come back home, we're going to be spending lots of time together," she says. "Just the way we always did. We'll talk and have a lot of fun, the way we used to."

I have no idea what my mother is talking about. She seems to be overlooking the fact that we've never spent much time together and we've never been close. Maybe, since I've ruined my life, she thinks that I'm more like her and we'll be a lot closer. "I can hardly wait to see you," she says before she hangs up.

That leaves me with my father. Over the phone his voice sounds different. Everything about him sounds different. He usually dominates most conversations because he's very witty and he tells lots of great stories. But today he's not talking much and his voice sounds as if it's coming from the moon. He doesn't sound that interested.

For years he and I were close. He was interested in everything I did. Every time I made good grades or won some kind of academic prize, he was happy. Sometimes I thought he was even happier than I was when I did well.

One time I heard my father joke that I made up for his not having a son. Maybe that was supposed to be a compliment. I don't know. For some reason it made me feel bad. But that doesn't matter now. We aren't close any longer. That's over. I read that in his letters, and I'm hearing it on the phone right now. There doesn't seem to be anything left between us.

More than anything, I know, my father hates weakness. He hates it in himself and in other people. And failure—I can't forget failure. My father hates that, too. I can't imagine anything that shows more weakness and more failure than what I've done. I loved someone who didn't love me back. I was weak and I got pregnant. None of this would have happened if I'd been a son.

"Do you have enough money?" my father asks. "Should I send you some more?"

"Thanks, but I don't need it," I say. "There's no place to spend it around here."

After a few minutes that seem to last forever, we say good-bye. When I hang up, I feel worse than I have in weeks.

I wake up Monday feeling horrible. I lie in bed for a long time, and I can't get up. I feel as if someone's pulled a black curtain over me. It stretches across my heart and it squeezes me and won't let go. I don't want to move or eat or talk. I hurt all over.

I felt this terrible once before in my life, after Jake broke up with me. All of a sudden I understood why people commit suicide. They felt the same kind of pain and blackness I was feeling, and they had to rip it out, because they couldn't stand it any longer. If that meant they had to kill themselves, who cared? The pain was unbearable, and they had to get rid of it any way they could.

It wasn't one of those things I wanted to understand, but I didn't have a choice. What was weird about it was that there was something comforting about knowing I could commit suicide. If everything became too hopeless, I had a way out. That wasn't something I went around telling people, of course. It wasn't the kind of thing I could bring up at the dinner table after Pamela had finally exhausted her endless supply of cheerleading anecdotes. So I never told anyone.

Once I read an article about Sylvia Plath in a magazine. She was supposed to be a great poet, and then she killed herself when she was pretty young. She stuck her head in the oven and turned on the gas and died. The article was very tragic and it made me feel bad. Then some creepy woman wrote the magazine to say that sure, she wasn't a poet or anything. But at least she hadn't gone around sticking her head in an oven and leaving her two children orphaned the way that selfish Sylvia Plath had.

That's pretty typical. That's the way people feel about suicide. They don't understand it at all. That's why I never talk about it. I only think about it sometimes. Like this morning, while I lie in bed.

For a while I watch the clock on my dresser. It's eleven in the morning. I watch its hands move slowly, and I wonder how I'll manage to get through the next hour. Or the afternoon. Every time I hear the clock tick, it hurts. It reminds me of how slowly time is moving, and how many seconds and minutes and hours there are, and how horrible it is to be alive. I hate being alive. It's torture to be alive.

There's a knock at the door. I don't say anything. The door swings open, and I can see Mrs. Landing. She walks to my bed and feels my forehead.

"Are you sick?" she asks.

"Not sick," I say. "But I feel bad." I sound pathetic, I know. I hate that, but I can't help it.

Mrs. Landing goes to the window and pulls back the curtains. I squint in the light.

"You're getting up," she says, "and you're getting dressed and you're coming with me."

I spend the rest of the day with Mrs. Landing. She makes me ride with her while she drives into town and runs errands. I don't start feeling instantly wonderful, but at least I stop wanting to kill myself in the next five minutes. That's progress under the circumstances.

I roll down the car window and let the wind blow my hair. I watch the stubby trees whip by. They're still green, but they look weather-beaten and faded by the sun. The leaves never change around here until November. By then I'll be a month closer to having the baby. I wonder how I'll feel then.

"You know, Anne," Mrs. Landing says, "sometimes you remind me of myself when I was your age."

I don't know what to say. I hate it when adults say things like that. It's always someone you don't want to be like. I think Mrs. Landing is nice, but I don't want to be like her. I can't imagine spending year after year being around girls who are as miserable as I am and seeing so much unhappiness.

I heard a rumor that Mrs. Landing had a baby out of wedlock when she was a teenager and that's why she spends her life doing this. I don't know if it's true, but I think it's too gross to think about. I can't imagine Mrs. Landing being a teenager and having sex. It's very revolting. I wonder if that was before or after she got her glass eye.

But I have to answer her. So I say, "Why?"

"I liked to keep other people at a distance too," she says. "I was afraid they wouldn't like me. So I stayed quiet and watched. And when I said something, I made sure it was casual and funny and showed people how I didn't care about anything."

I'm beginning to regret riding with her. I don't want to spend the next several hours listening to some kind of half-baked mumbo jumbo about myself. So I don't say anything.

Neither does Mrs. Landing. I have to say one thing about her. She's different from most adults. She doesn't usually keep bugging you about things. She seems to know when you aren't going to listen to something, no matter how many times she repeats it. Sometimes she actually knows how to keep her mouth shut. That's amazing for someone her age.

She hardly says anything until a couple of hours later, when we're driving back to the home. "When you're feeling as bad as you were earlier," she says, "will you be able to talk to Mrs. Harris about it?"

"I've known barnyard animals that are smarter than Mrs. Harris," I say. "She should be put to sleep before she does any damage. I'd rather die than talk to her about anything."

"Well," Mrs. Landing says, "we can't pick our social workers. We have to take anyone the county wants to send us."

We reach the home, and she parks the car and turns off the ignition. "Do this for me," she says. "Will you come and talk to me if you ever feel that bad again?"

I say I will.

I feel better on Tuesday. But I'm nervous, too. I don't ever want to feel as bad again as I did yesterday. Those moods scare me. I'm afraid I'll get in one of those moods and it will never end. I'll be stuck there forever.

That's what happened to my mother. Before the doctor sent her to the hospital that year, I can remember coming home from school and how everything was silent and dark at our house. I'd think no one was home. But then I realized that of course my mother was there. Her car was in the driveway, and she never walked anywhere. So I'd look around the house and I'd finally find her upstairs in bed. She'd have the covers pulled up to her chin and she'd just be lying there, staring. She looked at me and sometimes it would seem to take her a few minutes to recognize me. Then she'd say she wasn't feeling well. Maybe if I left her alone, she'd feel better later.

I don't remember where Pamela was those afternoons. Maybe she was there, and I've just forgotten. All I can remember is how hushed the house was and how I didn't want to make any noise at all. The silence was even worse than the afternoons I came home and found my mother crying. At least then I knew she was alive.

Most evenings when my father came home, he walked into the bedroom to talk to my mother. I never heard what they were saying. There was just a soft murmur of voices and then he came out of the room and closed the door. He always had a sad, puzzled look on his face when he came out. That was strange. My father didn't spend much time looking puzzled or sad. He seemed to understand everything, and he always told Pamela and me that being happy was a choice. "If you're sad, you're choosing to be sad," he said. When I looked at him, I wondered if he was choosing to be sad. I didn't think so.

He came into the kitchen those nights, and he and Pamela and I made dinner together. It was usually something awful, like canned soup and crackers. We ate together at the kitchen bar, instead of in the dining room, and we did sloppy things like putting the milk carton right there in front of us. My mother never allowed us to do things like that.

I could tell how hard my father was trying those nights. He asked Pamela and me about school and he listened to us carefully. Then he talked about cases he was working on. Pamela and I answered, and the three of us tried to make conversation. But I knew that what we were doing was listening. Over the sounds of our own voices, we were listening to the silence in the house, and we were waiting for something to happen.

A few weeks later my mother went to the hospital. She was gone when I got home from school that day, and my father was there. I'd never seen him in the house that early on a weekday. Later he took Pamela and me to a drugstore and bought us ice-cream cones with double dips. I can still see those cones, with the ice cream melting down the side. Pamela and I tried to lick them, but they melted faster than we could keep up with and slid down onto our hands and made them pastel colored and sticky.

My father didn't get any ice cream. He sat and watched us quietly and finally he told us that Mother had gone to the hospital. "The doctors said she was very, very tired," he said. "They don't know how long she'll have to stay, but we won't worry about that. She'll stay in the hospital and have a wonderful rest. Then she'll come home—and she'll be herself again."

I concentrated on my ice cream because I didn't want to look at my father's face. I knew how sad he was, but I also knew he was lying. My mother didn't need a rest. She'd spent the last two months in bed. How could she be tired? I'd never heard of anyone going to the hospital for a rest. How could she sleep in the hospital? It was even noisier than our house.

But I knew that was all my father was going to say, and I knew enough not to ask any questions. Pamela started to cry. She said she missed Mother. Daddy patted her on her sticky hand and helped her wipe her face off.

Pamela cried about everything. But I didn't, especially

not then. Daddy had enough to worry about already. That afternoon I knew he was the only parent I had. I wanted to help him by not making a fuss and not asking questions he didn't want to answer.

Later in the week I go back to the group meeting. I've missed a bunch of days. While I was gone, some things changed.

"We're going to try to have a topic of discussion for each meeting," Mrs. Landing says. "This is a new idea that one of the girls suggested. It allows us to focus on some important issues we need to talk about. Maybe it will work and maybe it won't. We'll try to be a little more organized and see how that goes."

She doesn't say who came up with that bright idea, but I suspect it's Rachel. She's still trying to boss us all around. I can imagine the topics Rachel will come up with. Why Nuclear War Is Bad. How to Act Cool When You See a Celebrity in a Coffeehouse. Why Looking Ugly Is Liberated.

What annoys me about Rachel is how she thinks she has to lecture the rest of us. She thinks we're complete rubes who never read a newspaper and here she is, bringing us some very hot news about civilization and social change. I can tell she expects us to hang on every word and ask her advice about complicated things like how to let the hair on our legs grow out so we can braid it.

Rachel doesn't realize it, but we already know about all the stuff she's blabbing about. We've all heard about communes and marijuana and hippies and LSD. Most of us know about someone's older sister or brother who went off to college and came home looking like a zombie and made it a point not to use deodorant because body odor is natural and beautiful. We've heard about people who had "bad trips" and ended up in insane asylums for the rest of their lives.

We've seen antiwar demonstrations on TV, the kind that made my father throw things and threaten to move our whole family to Australia. (People were still normal in Australia, he said. Australians knew how important it was to fight in Vietnam, and they weren't a bunch of cowards, either. Or maybe it was New Zealand. He'd find out from his travel agent.) We even know about draft dodgers and conscientious objectors and people who go to Canada so they won't get drafted. We know about it all. So what?

Rachel hinted one day that she'd smoked marijuana. I guess that was supposed to knock our socks off. Harriet, Cheryl's Bible-thumping friend, says she knows for a fact Rachel was lying about that.

"You can always tell when someone's taken drugs," Harriet says. "Their pupils stay dilated for the rest of their lives. Have you noticed Rachel's pupils? They're the size of pinpricks, so she must be lying." Harriet announces she's praying for Rachel anyway, because she can tell Rachel needs to know the Lord. After all, lying is just about as bad as drug taking, Harriet says.

I don't think that Rachel's lying about anything,

exactly. But I'm not sure she believes everything she says. She gets excited and talks and talks about the war and California and social change, and sometimes that makes me think she's talking so she won't have to think about something. I'm that way too. When I don't want to think about something, I read a lot. I'm taking a correspondence course in government, and I'd rather read about very boring things like the electoral college and democracy than think about being pregnant. I like being bored a lot more than I like feeling sad.

At least I only bore myself, though. Rachel likes to bore everyone around her. She never seems to notice that no one's listening. That's a common occurrence around here. We either have big talkers (LaNelle, Nancy, Rachel, and Donna) or people who never say anything (me, Cheryl, Gracie). That's what Mrs. Landing mentions today.

"You know, some of you never say anything at these meetings," she says. "And others of you dominate the conversations. That's one reason we're going to choose a new topic every day. Maybe that way we can encourage more of you to talk."

Today's topic, Mrs. Landing tells us, is how we found out about the facts of life. Oh, brother. I wonder whose stupid idea that is. I can't think of anything I'm less interested in talking about.

"Some parents never talk to their children about sex or menstruation," Mrs. Landing is saying. "Some of them do, but they're embarrassed or they act as if sex is something to be ashamed of. Most of us get our feelings about sex from our parents, and I think it's important to look at that."

She finishes talking and looks around the group encouragingly. Dead silence. If Mrs. Landing hadn't been so nice to me this week, I would think it's pretty funny. As it is, I'm embarrassed for her. I hope someone will say something soon. Not me, of course. Someone else.

The silence drags on, and then Mrs. Landing finally says, "Cheryl, do you have anything to say? Can you tell us how your parents talked to you about the facts of life?"

Cheryl turns beet red, all the way up to her reddish hairline. I've finally figured out that she's as shy as I am, and I can tell she's about to die of embarrassment. I almost expect her to get up and run from the room, but she doesn't.

"Well," she says after a long pause, "no one ever told me anything. We never talked about sex at my house, ever. I'm the oldest kid in the family, so I didn't have older brothers or sisters to tell me anything. I was thirteen when I got my period. I thought I was sick, and I told my mother I needed to go to the hospital. That must sound funny now to all of you, but I didn't know what was wrong with me. I thought maybe I was dying."

Cheryl's mother gave her sanitary pads, she says, and she lectured her about "keeping herself clean." But she didn't tell her anything about sex and having babies.

"I didn't find out about that till I was sixteen and I got pregnant." Cheryl starts to cry all of a sudden. "I thought you had to be married to have babies. That's how stupid I was. I thought you had to love each other."

"Cheryl, you weren't stupid—not at all," Mrs. Landing tells her. "It wasn't your fault your parents didn't tell you about the facts of life. How could you have known?" But Cheryl keeps on crying anyway.

"That's the problem with the South," Rachel says. You can tell she's been dying to jump in with that conclusion. If there's a problem on Jupiter, Rachel would blame it on the South. "People here don't like to acknowledge sex," she says. "That's why there are so many unwanted pregnancies in this area."

"As far as I can tell, the only thing Californians do is acknowledge sex," Nancy snaps. "They talk about it all the time and have sex with complete strangers in public parks and peace marches. If that's so great, how did you get pregnant, Rachel? And what are you doing here?"

So much for organized meetings. Rachel and Nancy continue to bicker, and Cheryl's crying in earnest now. Mrs. Landing moves next to her and talks to her quietly.

The rest of us sit there and say nothing, as usual. I think about how my mother talked to me about sex the year my period started. I was thirteen, like Cheryl. My mother told me I was a woman now and that was wonderful.

After that she told me about all kinds of strange things like penises and vaginas, and she used the word *intercourse*. I tried to imagine it. Intercourse. The way I imagined it, the man came up and stuck his penis in you and then he walked off.

That didn't sound great to me. It sounded kind of like having a shot. I could tell it wasn't going to be a problem for me to avoid intercourse until I got married. After that, I just hoped you didn't have to do it too often.

The Ninth Week
October 15-21

I have a dream about Jake on Wednesday night. It's the first time I've dreamt about him since I came here.

In the dream he's close to me, and all I can see is his face. I loved his face. I loved to touch it and feel the tiny stubble on his cheeks. I loved to kiss him and rub my face against his.

That's what we're doing in the dream, kissing and looking at each other and kissing again. I feel warm and happy, the way I did when we first started dating. But then his face begins to disappear. I reach out to touch his cheek, and I can't feel anything. Or maybe he's there, but he's getting farther and farther away. I keep asking him where he is, but I can't hear him answer. My own voice gets louder and louder, but no one answers.

Finally I wake up. I've been talking in my sleep. Wonderful. That proves I'm going crazy.

I'm glad that Cheryl's already gone to wherever she goes in the morning, prayer group or something. She invited me to it once a few weeks ago. I told her I'd rather sleep than pray any day. She didn't think that was funny, and she never mentioned it again.

I've always heard you're supposed to think about your dreams and figure out what they mean. The trouble is I have very basic, boring dreams. I wonder if that means I'm shallow. Shallow and screwed up is a pathetic combination. I want to think I'm deep and screwed up, at the very least.

Take this dream, for instance. It would take a moron about ten seconds to figure it out. Jake was with me and then he left me. But I still love him. That's the part that kills me—I still love him. It makes me think I don't even have basic survival instincts. If I was smart at all, I would hate him for not loving me. But I don't. Sometimes I think it makes me love him more. Maybe I'm some kind of masochist, along with being passive-aggressive. It's not a pretty picture.

I wasn't even surprised when Jake broke up with me. I knew it was coming. At first he called every day, and sometimes more. We were together all the time. That all changed after we'd been sleeping together for a few weeks. A day or two would pass and he wouldn't call. Sometimes I'd get so eager to hear his voice that I'd call him. I knew that was a big mistake, but I did it anyway. My mother always said that only girls with no pride called boys. That was me, I knew. Once I'd had a lot of pride, but now it was gone, kaput, nonexistent. It went down the toilet, right along with my virginity.

Jake sounded funny when I called, even though he always said he was glad to hear from me. We'd usually go out soon after we talked. Well, it wasn't going out anymore. It was going to have sex in the car. I wanted to talk with him and go places with him and be together. But we just had sex. That had seemed to make him happy, at first. But even that wore off. We were having sex, me to please him and him to please himself—but he didn't seem to be that pleased any longer. I wondered what I'd done wrong.

I didn't want to face what was happening. I knew he'd finally figured out that I wasn't worth loving. There wasn't much I could do about that. I wondered why it had taken him so long to figure it out.

For a few weeks he was closer to me than anyone had ever been. In a way I felt like he'd looked inside me. He'd seen what I was really like, and now he wanted to leave. I could understand. That was the big joke, that I could understand his wanting to leave. I couldn't even blame him for it.

He broke up with me one evening in May. May 14, to be exact—I always remember dates of bad things that happen to me. It was raining that night, and we'd driven to the park to have sex, and then he drove me home. We sat there for a few minutes in front of my house. He told me he thought we were getting too serious. He wanted us to be friends, he said. But he thought we should see other people.

I sat and stared straight ahead and watched the wind-
shield wipers move back and forth. Maybe if I look at
them long enough, I thought, I'll get hypnotized. Back
and forth, back and forth, all the time he was talking to
me. It takes a long time to be hypnotized. I had to be
patient. I had to concentrate. I had to give it time.

I turned my face to Jake finally. He looked uncomfortable. But the worst thing was when he stared back at me.
There was something hard and set in his eyes, and it
made me realize that I wasn't anything to him anymore.
Maybe he'd liked me once. Or maybe not. Maybe I'd just
wanted to believe it so badly that I'd thought it was true.

His eyes were cold and calm. It didn't matter what I
did or said. I was nothing to him.

So this is what it feels like to have your heart break,
I thought. I don't know why I was thinking that, because
I couldn't feel anything.

I didn't want to look at Jake any longer, because I
knew I couldn't stand the coldness in his eyes. I slid
across the seat and opened the door and got out without
saying anything. I walked slowly up our driveway, getting
drenched by the rain, and I heard his car pull away. I
didn't look back at him.

For a long time I sat on our front porch and stared
out into the night and the rain and blurred streetlights.
But I didn't see anything. I sat there for a long time, and I
can't remember getting up and going inside and going
to bed.

It was days later before it occurred to me that Jake
hadn't even bothered to turn off the car and the wind-

shield wipers when he talked to me. He'd known it wouldn't take long.

On Saturday I have my second doctor's visit. The doctor who comes here is young and good looking. He has honey-colored hair and blue-green eyes, and some of the girls call him Dr. Kildare. On his name tag it says DR. BLANCHARD. I'd like to know what his first name is. Thomas, maybe? I like the name Thomas. It sounds good with Blanchard. Thomas Blanchard, M.D.

I'm now almost seven months pregnant and I've gained twelve pounds. "That's perfect," Thomas says.

He places the stethoscope on my stomach. "I'm sorry it's so cold," he says, smiling. He actually looks concerned about it. He's a wonderful, caring doctor, I can tell.

"The baby's heartbeat sounds good and strong," he says. "Do you want to hear it?"

I don't, but I can't say no. I lean closer so I can hear.

The baby's heartbeat is fast. It sounds like a gallop. It makes me feel strange suddenly to hear the baby. I close my eyes while I listen, and I find myself wondering what the baby looks like. The baby whose heart I'm hearing.

I haven't read anything about a baby's development in a long time. I haven't wanted to. But now I start to wonder. Does it have hair? Fingernails? Can it think? Can it feel anything?

For a few seconds I can almost see the baby floating around inside me. Its eyes are closed, and it's warm and comfortable and protected. I'm keeping it safe. I'm taking care of it.

I feel like I'm going to cry. I've heard the baby and I've seen it, kind of, and I know I don't want that. It was so much better when I thought of it as a tumor, like something mean and malignant.

For weeks, though, I haven't thought of it as a tumor or any kind of growth. I've tried not to think about it at all. That's worked pretty well. I like not thinking about things. It helps sometimes. It means I can have a few days when I don't feel awful. I can spend my time reading books and studying for my correspondence class and going to group meetings. I wouldn't call myself happy. I've hardly ever been happy in my life, though, and this isn't bad.

But now I've started thinking about the baby, and seeing it, and I know I can't stop.

Like I said, I'm a very obsessive person. I saw an article about obsessive people last week in an old issue of *Time* that Mrs. Landing had. It called those people "obsessive-compulsive." They spend their lives washing their hands about a hundred times a day or making sure the TV set is turned off even if they don't have a TV.

If I'm going to be an obsessive-compulsive person, I wish I'd concentrate on something like that. Washing your hands isn't so bad. At least you're very clean. As far as I can tell, it beats the hell out of thinking about a baby no one wants.

I don't want to think about that baby at all. I hadn't wanted it. No one wanted it.

The baby sprang to life—when? Well, sometime in April. Jake and I were probably in his 1965 red LeMans.

We rolled around in the backseat for several minutes one night in April.

April. Spring. April love. Stars and flowers and fresh breezes and romance and soft music and a boy and a girl. It sounds so beautiful and so wonderful. But it wasn't like that at all.

What it was, really, is the story of a lonely girl in that car. It didn't matter what she had to do, because she would have done anything. She wanted to be held and to feel loved for a few minutes, even though she knew she wasn't lovable, that she was only fooling herself.

It seemed sad to me then, and it seems even sadder now. Like I said, I feel like I'm a hundred years old most days. I can't figure out how that girl and boy in the car made something that's still alive. When I feel the baby move, it always surprises me. I've felt dead for so long that I can't believe there's life anywhere.

It's Saturday night, and Cheryl seems as depressed as I am. We're beginning to talk about it when Nancy comes barging in our room. She doesn't knock, of course. She never knocks.

Just the sight of her irritates me. Her blond hair is in a perfect flip as usual, and I still can't see any roots showing. She wears makeup every day, like she's going out on a hot date—blue eye shadow and lots of mascara and pastel lipstick. I've heard that pregnant women often start to look puffy and they get big, purple varicose veins. I can hardly wait for Nancy to start looking puffy. Maybe she'll have to wear support hose for her varicose veins, and her hair may start falling out soon. That happens a lot when you're pregnant, too.

Nancy never seems to notice that she irritates me. She always assumes that everyone on earth is as madly in love with her as she is with herself.

I wonder what it's like to feel good, the way Nancy does. I want to know what it's like to look perfect and like yourself the way you are instead of always trying to change, the way I do. It must be a nice feeling. I've never felt that way. I don't think I ever will.

Nancy plops down on Cheryl's bed and announces she's having a party in her room that night.

"It's been pretty boring around here," she says, "so I thought I'd liven things up a little. My room, seven o'clock. Chips, dips, and a little something special for all of us. Come as you are, of course," she adds breezily. "No use in getting dressed up, since there aren't any men around."

She winks at us broadly and waltzes out. She looks proud of herself, the way she always does, like she's given us a great present or something. Nancy's still confusing this place with a sorority house. She's been here for almost a month now, and she hasn't figured it out. Rachel calls her the Sweetheart of Sigma Nu sometimes. Nancy corrects her and says it's Sigma Chi, not Sigma Nu. That usually eggs Rachel on. Sometimes I think Rachel's passive-aggressive too. When she isn't talking about California, she's not so bad.

I hate to admit it, but I'm happy to get out of our room. I'd go anywhere to get away. I might go completely nuts if I stay here much longer and think about the baby. Every time it moves, I "see" it. I'm sure this is very unhealthy behavior. I'm getting as crazy as everyone else here.

So Cheryl and I go to Nancy's party. I pull on a sweat-shirt and some blue jeans with an elastic waist. The jeans are getting tighter, and I don't know how much longer I'll be able to get into them. Cheryl puts on a big, plaid tent dress that Mrs. Landing lent her. Whoever it belonged to originally must have had quadruplets. It makes Cheryl look like a plaid bowling ball.

When we get to Nancy's room, she's lit lots of candles that smell funny—like gardenias, maybe. That must be very exotic in Mississippi. She's also poured a bunch of potato chips into blue Tupperware bowls, and there are some plastic containers with French onion dip in them. There are already several girls in the room, even though it's barely seven. Everybody else must be as hard up as Cheryl and I are.

Nancy's room is a lot more decorated than ours. She has about a million stuffed animals on her bed—pandas and poodles and even a big green giraffe. We already know all about her stupid stuffed animals. "Every one of them is from one of my boyfriends," she said when she moved in. "I left most of 'em back in Mississippi, though." I didn't know if she was talking about her stuffed animals or her boyfriends, and I didn't ask. Every time I look at those animals, I wonder what Nancy had to do to earn them.

Rachel's sitting on Nancy's bed, next to a red poodle

with a pink tongue. She looks comfortable and settled in, which surprises me. Nancy must be desperate if she invited Rachel. But Nancy's one of these people who have to invite absolutely everybody. She can't stand not to have a crowd around.

Rachel is as big as a house now. She looks like some kind of black-haired Buddha sitting on the bed, with her hands folded on her stomach. She's wearing one of those long dresses, as usual. They're called caftans, she's told us at least six hundred times. Everyone in California wears caftans these days, she says.

Harriet, the religious nut, is sitting on the floor. She looks wispy as usual. Every time I see her, I wonder how she managed to get pregnant. I can't imagine Harriet having sex. Maybe those old-wives' stories about toilet seats are true. Maybe she picked the wrong toilet seat and she got pregnant from it. Not that I can imagine Harriet on a toilet seat either.

Harriet is always talking about "the Lord," which is one reason I try not to be around her much. She goes around saying things like, "When I was talking to the Lord this morning, he told me to take out the trash." Well, not that bad, actually, but you get the point. The Lord seems to take a personal interest in every little thing that Harriet does.

I wonder if anyone ever told Harriet that hearing voices is a sign of mental derangement. I also wonder what the Lord said when she got pregnant out of wedlock. He probably warned her to always spread toilet paper on the seat, and now look what happened. I bet

He gave her the silent treatment for about a week after that.

I look around the room and notice that Gracie's here too. That's amazing. I haven't seen Gracie anywhere in days, and now I understand why. She looks awful. She has dark circles under her eyes, and her skin is so pale and thin, you feel like you can almost see through it, like one of those baby birds that don't have feathers yet.

Sometimes when I see Gracie, it hurts to look at her. The rest of us seem to have grown up—or grown old— overnight. But not Gracie. She looks like a puzzled child. The bigger her stomach gets, the smaller the rest of her seems, and the younger she looks.

I can't imagine how Nancy got Gracie to come to this party. Then I remember that the two of them are roommates. (Good Lord. No wonder Gracie looks so bad.) Nancy probably went around inviting people to their room and didn't bother to tell Gracie. That's typical of Nancy's selfish behavior. Maybe, when she isn't looking, I'll find her Vaseline and hide it. Then she'll develop lots of stretch marks.

"Look what I've got for us!" That's Nancy, yelling. Her southern-fried accent has gotten thicker all of a sudden. She holds up two big jugs of wine like they're trophies.

"We can get plastered!" she announces. The way she's talking, I'm pretty sure she's already halfway there. She twists the top off one bottle and starts pouring it into paper cups and spilling the rest. The wine looks like cherry Kool-Aid. Actually it tastes like cherry Kool-Aid, but it's a lot sweeter.

I've never drunk much before. But tonight I want to. I want to forget about everything. I want to fly. I know that drinking is against the rules here and we'll probably all get in trouble, but I don't care.

"Bottoms up!" Nancy says, and I slowly drain the wine from my cup. I'm not the only one, I notice. Even Cheryl is sipping hers. And Gracie, too. Gracie is probably ten years under the legal drinking age. I bet it's a felony for her to even be around the stuff.

"I don't drink," Harriet says. "It's against my religion. Do you have any milk?"

"We're out in the country," Nancy retorts. "Go find a cow." She bends over one of the candles and lights a cigarette and throws back her head and inhales it in a loud rush of air. "God," she says, "it's been too long since I've had one of these."

"You'll stunt your growth," Rachel says.

"Big deal," Nancy shrugs. "I'm already as tall as I want to be. Besides, the only people who don't smoke in college are losers. You'll find out when you get there."

She puts her cigarette in a cup she's using as an ashtray and holds up a deck of cards. "Anyone want to play poker?" she asks. "Five-card draw. We're going to use buttons for chips."

"I'm leaving," Harriet says.

"Too bad," Nancy says. "We're certainly going to miss you." She sits down and starts shuffling the cards very professionally between drags on her cigarette and gulps of wine. She seems to be experienced at all three. Out of the corner of my eye I see Harriet inching toward the door. She seems to be waiting for someone to ask her not to leave, but no one does.

Nancy deals the cards to Gracie, Rachel, Cheryl, and me. I've never played poker before. I've never done a lot of things. But I don't let that stop me. I pour some more wine and start to play. Every time it's my turn, I take as many cards as I can and I always bet a thousand dollars in buttons. Sometimes I win, and I'm not sure why. But I keep on playing.

We play hand after hand, and I finally figure out that being drunk may not be the best state to learn something in. I still don't know what the rules are. So I roll over on my back and throw my cards up in the air. "I'm quitting while I'm ahead!" I screech.

My cards fly everywhere. Then Rachel throws her cards at Nancy, and Cheryl flings a pillow. I don't know who she's aiming at. She almost falls over when she heaves it over her head. "Tim-ber!" she says.

We're all laughing and throwing things. For once I feel like I'm part of a group. I like everybody here, I think suddenly. We're all friends. A card lands on Gracie's head, and she pulls it off and smiles. She looks almost cheerful.

"We should tell fortunes now!" Nancy says. "I'm great at telling fortunes!" She moves around the room unsteadily, trying to pick up the cards. They slip out of her hands.

"I can tell fortunes too," I say. I haven't talked this much since I've been in the home. In the back of my mind, I hope I'm making sense. I reach down to the floor and pull up a card. I point at Rachel. "You're going to have a baby! That's your fortune!"

We all think that's hysterical. I've never rolled on the floor with laughter before, but I'm close to it now. Everything is so funny. Everything I say is witty. Even Gracie is giggling. Or maybe she has the hiccups.

"And now I'm going to read your past," I tell Cheryl. I pull up another card and peer at it and try to focus my eyes. It's the king of spades. He looks mean and dumb. "You've got a mean, dumb son of a bitch in your past!" I say.

Cheryl looks surprised for a minute. Then she laughs uneasily, along with everyone else.

I pick up another card from the floor. The seven of clubs. Who cares? "You've got a son of a bitch in your past!" I announce, pointing at Nancy. "And you too!" I say to Rachel. "And so do I!" I'm drunk, but I'm not drunk enough to say anything to Gracie. I don't want to insult her father, do I? Or maybe I do. I'm not sure. I pour myself another cup of wine and try to remember to keep my mouth shut after this.

"We've all got sons of bitches in our past," Cheryl says. I've never heard her say a word like that, ever. Once she stubbed her toe on the bureau and it was all bloody and disgusting, and all she said was "Dang it." But now here she is, looking flushed and angry. She pours herself some more wine too.

"Let's toast all the sons of bitches we know," she says.

"To all the bastards in the world!" Nancy shrieks. She's

a lot drunker than the rest of us, I can tell. For once her hair is a little messy.

We're all laughing hysterically, but something seems different all of a sudden. There's some kind of bitterness in the air. It reminds me of the time my mother accidentally set her hair on fire with a cigarette lighter. Like then, there's a nasty smell that's lingering here.

We raise our cups together. "To Jake, that piece of shit," I say. I can't believe I said that. I've never even mentioned Jake's name here. But I like the way the toast sounds.

"To David!" Rachel says. "He's a piece of shit too." Her voice is louder than usual but it sounds ragged, like she has a cold.

"To all the men on earth!" Nancy yells. "They're shitheads!"

We touch our cups together and bright red wine splashes everywhere. Gracie is sitting a few feet away, but she raises her cup too. We drink noisily, and then there's a short silence.

Cheryl raises her cup. "To William Browning," she says. She's speaking slowly and deliberately, I realize, so she won't mispronounce the name. She has tears in her eyes, but the others don't seem to notice. They're too busy drinking and toasting.

"To my parents," Rachel says. Her voice sounds normal now. "They can get screwed and die." We toast. "To this whole nasty, evil society," Rachel goes on. We toast the nasty, evil society. It seems like the friendly thing to do, even if the rest of us don't believe it. We also toast Lyndon Johnson. "That fascist pig," Rachel calls him.

I swallow the last drops of wine in my cup. I've lost count of how much I've drunk, but I know it's a lot. I've gone from feeling buoyant to feeling dizzy and sick. Rachel's fallen back on the bed with her eyes closed. Gracie's lying on the floor, all curled up. She's asleep.

Nancy pulls a blanket off her bed and stumbles toward Gracie. She covers Gracie with the blanket and tucks it all around her. When she sees Cheryl and me watching her, she gives us a sheepish smile. "Sometimes I feel like Gracie's mother," she says.

Nancy picks up her cup again and raises it. "Let's make more toasts!" she says. But Cheryl and I are already standing up, sort of, to leave. It's hard to stand upright and it's harder to walk. "We've got to leave before we pass out," I tell Nancy. Nancy shrugs and spills more wine.

Cheryl and I grope our way to the door. When I turn around, I see Nancy pouring herself another glass of wine. The bottle's almost empty.

By the time we get to our room, I feel sick. I fall on my bed and lie there and watch the room move. I close my eyes so that everything will stand still.

"Who's Jake?" Cheryl asks. Her voice comes out of the darkness a few feet away. I open my eyes and I can see her silhouetted against the window.

"Jake," I whisper. "Jake, Jake, Jake." It's funny to pronounce his name out loud again. It's also hard. I have to work at it. It's a tongue twister.

"I loved Jake. Who was Jake? I don't know. He wasn't

who I wanted him to be. Jake, Jake, Jake." I say his name again and again. It sounds like a song.

I can see Jake's face in the dark, looking at me. God, I loved him. There's a big black hole where my heart used to be, and I don't think it will ever stop hurting. I called him a piece of shit tonight, but I don't feel like that any longer. I'm the one who's the piece of shit.

I feel tears in my eyes for the second time today. If I don't watch it, I'm going to be an even bigger mess. I'll be crying twenty-four hours a day, and I'll have to be institutionalized. I have to stop crying. I have to stop thinking, too.

"Who's William Browning?" I ask Cheryl.

She doesn't answer for several minutes, and I think she's fallen asleep. So I lie there and don't say anything and start to drift off to sleep myself.

"He was my pastor," I think I hear Cheryl say before I start to dream.

The Tenth Week
October 22-28

Mrs. Landing found out about the party and all the drinking we did. She always finds out about everything eventually.

We all think it's Harriet who told her. Harriet probably spent the day praying for all of us to suffer and then she went off and told Mrs. Landing, just in case the Lord didn't punish us fast enough.

So Mrs. Landing called Cheryl, Nancy, Rachel, and me into her office Monday morning. She didn't ask to see Gracie. She must have thought Gracie was an innocent victim, since she's too young to know better.

"All of you know the rules in this home," Mrs. Landing says. She looks from face to face. "You know liquor isn't allowed here. I'm very disappointed in all of you."

Cheryl is squirming and Rachel looks a little green and sick. But the talk doesn't seem to bother Nancy much. I have a feeling she's heard something like this before.

No matter what she's saying, I don't think Mrs. Landing is as mad as she pretends to be. She's fiddling with her glasses a lot, pushing them farther up on her nose. She's trying hard to frown and sound mean and angry. But she's not convincing.

The only thing that kills me is when Mrs. Landing says she'll have to put a note in Mrs. Harris's files about the party. "Mrs. Harris has to be notified about things like this," she says.

Great. Just great. That's all I need. That old biddy Harris will jump on this like a dog in heat. She'll love the chance to talk to me about my future as an alcoholic, and how she can tell I need a lot of help from someone kind and understanding, like her. If there's anyone who can drive me to alcoholism, it's Mrs. Harris. Maybe I'll tell her I've been drinking since I was in the first grade. It started when I used to put vodka in my paste jars.

"That's all I have to say," Mrs. Landing says. "Unless any of you want to tell me anything?"

We don't, of course. We leave her office, and the four of us walk outside and sit on the porch.

The weather is cool and beautiful. The sky's a deep, sparkling blue, and the sun is bright. I love fall. It always seems so invigorating after the long, sweaty summers we have in Texas. Every year when fall comes, I think that something exciting is about to happen. Even this year, when I know for a fact that nothing good is going to happen to me, I still feel better when the weather turns.

We sit on the porch and don't say anything. Rachel is squinting in the bright light, and Nancy looks cross. Cheryl has her chin on her hand, and she's staring off into the distance. I can't imagine what she's looking at. There's nothing to see but a few twisted mesquite trees and a sky that stretches on forever.

Cheryl's been avoiding me since Saturday night, when she told me who William Browning is. I feel bad about that, because she and I usually talk every day. I want to make her feel better, but I don't know what to say. Sometimes I don't know the right thing to say, and I end up making things worse. So I haven't said anything.

I understand why she's embarrassed about having sex with a minister, though. I can't imagine sleeping with a minister. I've never seen one yet who's even remotely attractive. I bet this guy was old, too, and maybe bald. I wonder if he raped Cheryl—like Gracie had been raped by her father. Or maybe they were praying together and he jumped on her and said it was the Lord's will that they have sex. He probably still had his robe on when he did it.

They call it "fornication" in the Bible. That's another reason why I hate the Bible. It uses words like *fornicate* that are a lot worse than anything you ever see on a bathroom stall. And then God gets pissed off and he throws lightning bolts or makes it flood or tries to talk you into killing your own kid.

I think the Bible is revolting. I'm sure you can find any kind of perversion you want in it. William Browning probably jumped on Cheryl while he quoted some verse from the Bible about how you're supposed to spread your legs for your minister so you could receive the Holy Ghost by special delivery.

That's typical of religion, if you ask me. No wonder Cheryl's so embarrassed and she can't talk to me. She was looking for the Holy Ghost, and all she got was screwed.

Unfortunately Mrs. Landing hasn't given up on that stupid idea of having topics for our meetings. The subject she comes up with on Wednesday is a winner as usual.

"Let's talk about how you got pregnant," she says. "Think about whether you wanted to make love—or did you just get yourself talked into it?"

She looks around the group and nods at us encouragingly. Nobody says anything. "Did you even know you could get pregnant by making love?" she asks. "And did you enjoy it? Or did you just do it to please your boyfriends?"

My God. Talk about personal questions. This is every bit as bad as something Rachel said last week. "In California lots of women get together in a circle, and they use hand mirrors and look at their own genitals," she said. Rachel said she thought that was a great idea, although she hadn't gotten around to doing it just yet.

"Why not, Rachel, if it's such a great idea?" Nancy asked.

Rachel didn't say anything. It was strange, because she loved fighting with Nancy. But this time she started crying all of a sudden, and no one knew why. Then she walked off and she didn't talk to any of us for a day or so.

Since then, no one's been arguing much. Someone told me that pregnant women get calmer the closer they are to having their babies. It has to do with hormones, as usual. When you're very pregnant, you have a bunch of hormones that slow you down and make you feel content. Maybe that's what's happening to all of us. We'll get more and more sluggish and we'll just sit around and eat and fall asleep with big grins on our faces all the time. That must be why I like everyone more these days. It's my hormones.

"Would anyone like to start the discussion on this?" Mrs. Landing asks. I sit on my hands, as usual. Not me! Not me!

Nancy wants to talk, of course. "I think I'm probably different from the rest of you," she says. "I like sex. I think it's fun. I've enjoyed myself."

She looks at the rest of us defiantly, like she expects us to jump in and correct her. No one says anything, so she goes on. "I've never let a man talk me into sex, and I never will. I did it because I wanted to. I made one stupid mistake that I'll never forgive myself for. I didn't use my diaphragm once, and I got pregnant."

Nancy shakes her blond hair back from her face. It flips perfectly, as always. She must use a ton of hairspray every day. She seems to be daring us to say something.

"A lot of this is a much bigger deal to the rest of you than it is to me," she says. "I didn't care about the guy I was with. He wasn't anyone I'd ever think about marrying. He was just a good time for me. Ten years from now he'll still be working as a mechanic and he won't even bother to clean his fingernails. He'll be married with a bunch of kids and for a really big night out, he and his wife will take them to the local cafeteria. He was a nice guy and he was fun, but I wouldn't think about marrying him in a million years. He never had any idea I was pregnant, and he'll never find out about this baby."

Nancy's finished. We all look at her and she stares back, still defiant.

She's right, I think, feeling surprised. Nancy's absolutely right. She *is* different from the rest of us. She's tougher than we are, and she knows what she's doing. She's smarter than the rest of us, too. That's funny to think about. I've always thought that being smart is the most important thing in the world.

In a way I have to admire Nancy for being smart and for figuring out things. I wish I could be like her, I think suddenly. I'd like to be tougher and smarter about life, the way she is. I don't want to care as much as I do. I'm tired of feeling hurt all the time. I'd rather be Nancy than me any day.

When Nancy talks about men, it's the same way my father talks about deer when he goes hunting in the fall. I can see Nancy on some kind of hunting preserve, carrying a gun. She's going after very big game marked "Future Doctor" or "Son of a Millionaire" or "Old Rich Guy with a Fatal Disease."

I can tell Nancy would never have a sudden attack of pity or remorse when she sights her prey. Why should she? she'd say. Since when have men ever taken pity on us?

Cheryl and I finally talk on Thursday. We're both in our room. I'm reading *Gone With the Wind* for the eighth or ninth time, I'm not sure which. I used to keep track of how many times I read it by marking the back cover. But then the cover fell off and I can't be sure any longer.

I read too much, my mother always told me. "Reading is fine, but it's not the same as living," she said.

She'd been out of the hospital two years when she said that, but she still had crazy spells. About once a month she'd start to look worse and worse, and she'd begin to pick at the rest of us. You couldn't even breathe right when she was in one of those moods. It was mostly me she was after. Pamela was gone a lot, and she didn't seem to be as angry at Pamela anyway. She didn't say much to my father, either. I had the feeling she was scared of him. Maybe she was afraid he'd leave her and she'd have to work for a living instead of playing bridge and going shopping and hanging around the church all the time.

So she'd start in on me, and she wouldn't leave me alone. I'd go to my room and close the door, but in a few minutes she'd follow me in. She'd sit on my bed and ask why I didn't want to talk to her. I'd finally put down my book and she'd start to tell me what was wrong with me. I read too much. I needed to get my hair cut. I wasn't nice enough to other people. I didn't pay attention in church. I wasn't a good Christian. I thought I was smart, but I wasn't smart in lots of important ways.

She'd talk on and on, and her eyes would get a vicious gleam in them. I wondered what I'd done to make her so angry at me. She'd end up screaming, and then I'd start to cry. She was nice to me then. Sometimes she patted my hair and hugged me, and told me she wanted me to do better and to be a better person so she wouldn't have to get so upset with me. She'd leave me alone for a few weeks until it started up again.

I never told my father about those times. I wouldn't have known how to describe them. All I knew was that I'd done something terrible and I'd made my mother very angry. Since I didn't understand it myself, it would have been impossible to explain to anyone else.

The stranger it got at our house, the more I read. I read everything I could lay my hands on—newspapers and magazines and books. I read good books like *The Diary of Anne Frank* and trashy books like *Forever Amber*. It didn't matter what I read, as long as it could make me disappear for a while. That's why I liked long books like *Gone With the Wind*. They helped me disappear for days. Sometimes I'd finish a book and turn right back to the front page and start reading again. It didn't matter where I was going, as long as I was gone.

Since I've been here, I haven't read as much. I think that's strange. I'm surprised I don't want to disappear into a book all the time. But I don't. Being at this home is like reading a book. Except this time I'm in it. I'm one of the damned characters. So is everybody else.

Maybe this place is like a mystery novel, where the most innocent-looking characters have the darkest secrets and probably killed the victim in the first scene, but it takes you hundreds of pages to figure it out. In that kind of book Cheryl and Gracie would be the murderers. They would have killed the victims with some kind of strange and devious weapon, like a stapler or a sharp bookmark.

I look at Cheryl, but I can't imagine her murdering anyone. Or Gracie, either. But Nancy. There's a murderer-in-training if I've ever seen one. I feel sorry for any rich guy who breaks off an engagement with her. She'll slit his jugular with her fingernail and walk away without needing a manicure.

But that's all beside the point. I have a tough time getting to the point these days. It must be another one of those hormonal things. I'll have to ask Thomas the next time I have an appointment with him.

Cheryl and I start to talk, and I put down my book. She says she's wondered why I haven't asked her more about William Browning.

"You must think I'm a terrible person for sleeping with my pastor," she says. "Do you want to change roommates?"

She's completely serious when she says that, and she watches me very closely.

"You're crazy—why would I think you're a terrible person for sleeping with a minister?" I say. "You're a friend, and I know you're a good person. I didn't say anything about it because I don't like to ask any questions that aren't any of my business." That isn't completely true. I'm perfectly happy to ask questions that aren't any of my business and to eavesdrop, too. But I haven't wanted to ask Cheryl any questions because I don't want to talk about Jake. It always seems to me that if anyone tells you a secret, then you're obligated to tell them one. And I don't want to do that.

"I'd like to hear about it if you want to tell me." But I'm not sure I want to hear what Cheryl is going to tell me. Except for Nancy and Rachel, everyone who talks here has a sad story. I think about what happened to me, and what I know about LaNelle and Donna and Gracie, and sometimes it's too much for me. It's too much sadness to hear again and again, and I feel like I'm suffocating.

Cheryl's face is starting to twitch, and I can tell she's about to cry. I want to be a good friend to her, but I'm not sure I want to be around for any kind of full-blown emotional crisis. I'm not good at emotional crises. They scare me. (Isn't that why this place brings in idiots like Mrs. Harris—so they can handle things like this? I hope they dock her pay every time someone has a breakdown around here.)

But Cheryl doesn't cry, fortunately. She just starts talking.

"Religion's always been important to me," she says. "My family was Southern Baptist. Most people in our town were. And we'd always gone to the Concord Street Baptist Church. Everyone was always friendly there, and it made me feel, I don't know, happy and peaceful, maybe, when I went there."

I can't imagine any church that could make me feel

happy and peaceful. Going to church makes me feel like I'm sitting on a cactus. I even hate organ music because it reminds me of churches. But I nod anyway.

"We got a new minister about two years ago," Cheryl says. "His name was Pastor Browning, and he was in his thirties. We'd never had such a young pastor before, and everyone loved him. His wife was young too, and their two kids were just adorable. When they came there, they put so much energy into the church. It was wonderful.

"So I started spending more and more time at the church. I helped with Sunday school and the children's choirs. I just felt happy every time I was there. I felt like everybody there liked me, especially Pastor Browning. He said I was one of the young people he'd come to depend on. He said he didn't worry about the future of the country when there were fine young people like me around."

Cheryl looks a little proud when she tells me that. I can understand. I still get happy for some reason when I think about my first dates with Jake. I know how stupid that is and I know how the story ends—but somehow I can always manage to forget for a few minutes. I feel like I've gone back in time and I can be happy again.

For a few minutes Cheryl's quiet, and she begins to look bleaker. "I went to the church a lot on Saturdays," she says. "Usually other people were there, like Mrs. Browning. We'd help clean the church or sometimes we'd put up special decorations if it was an important day like Easter. But one Saturday I went there and everyone had gone home early. Pastor Browning and I were the only ones there.

"We worked together and we cleaned up the sanctuary. I was using one of those big, wide brooms like janitors have, pushing all the dirt and dust into a pile. It was hot that day, so I had on a T-shirt and jeans. If you were a Baptist in my town, you never wore shorts. It didn't matter how hot it got. After a while, Pastor Browning said we'd both been working so hard, we should rest some. So we sat down on the floor. Both of us were all dusty and dirty, and we laughed about that.

"You know what's funny about this?" Cheryl asks. She stares at me, but I can tell she isn't seeing me. "I was sitting there, talking and laughing with him, and I kept thinking that I wished my dad had been like Pastor Browning. Sometimes I even pretended that he was my father. I thought it would be wonderful to have a father like him. You know, I could tell he liked me and he thought I was something special. So I'd pretend for a few minutes that he was my dad. Except I never could imagine what it'd be like to have a father who liked you."

Cheryl's sitting on her bed while she says this. She's drawn up her legs and she has her arms wrapped around them. She puts down her head so I can't see her face anymore, but she continues to talk.

"He told me I had a little dirt on my face," she says. "He took out his handkerchief and started cleaning it off. Then he dropped the handkerchief all of a sudden and he was touching my face, kind of softly. He told me he loved me. He couldn't stop himself, because he loved me. He started taking off his clothes and my clothes, and I didn't know what to do. He loved me! That was what he said!

"I know I should have stopped him, but I couldn't. I couldn't even say much. I kept saying no, and he'd say, Shhhhh, and put his finger across my lips, and there was still something so nice about him. I tried to think that it was all right, because I loved him too. But I knew it wasn't that kind of love. He said this was all good and right, because we loved each other. I knew it wasn't right, but I couldn't stop it.

"We were there for so long that it began to get dark. Then he started acting different. He pulled on his clothes, and he told me I needed to get dressed too. I hurt all over. When I was getting dressed, I noticed there was blood on the floor. He said we'd have to clean it up. He acted like it was just part of the dirt and dust we'd been sweeping up. He seemed like a different person. I was still sitting there on the floor, trying to pull my jeans on and every part of me hurt, and he told me I had to hurry up. He looked at me like I was some kind of tramp. He'd never looked at me like that before, and I didn't know where it had come from. I kept waiting for him to say something. I wanted him to tell me it'd be all right. But he didn't. He just wanted me to leave."

Cheryl lifts up her face. She isn't crying. She's staring at the wall now, talking in a funny monotone.

"I left there," she says, "and I knew I could never go back to that church. I knew I could never face him again.

I'd done something horrible. I didn't understand exactly what had happened, but I knew I'd sinned and it was my fault and God would punish me for it. That's why I'm pregnant. It's my punishment."

She's crying now, and I know I have to say something. All I can think is how much I hate religion and churches and ministers. I can see Pastor Browning up there, preaching hell and damnation and feeling himself under his big black robe. Ministers are creeps. Most of the ones I've known should be in cages at the zoo. I wonder why no one ever figures that out. Haven't they read *Elmer Gantry*?

"But it wasn't your fault," I answer finally. "The worst thing you did was trust him. Besides, pregnancy's not a punishment. It just happens. It was an accident."

I wish I could believe that, but I don't. I consider my own pregnancy my punishment for being stupid and weak. Every time I look down at myself and see how big I'm getting, it reminds me of what an idiot I've been. It's a message that gets louder every day.

"That's not what my parents said," Cheryl says. "They didn't believe a word of what I told them. They said I was accusing Pastor Browning—this fine, fine man, they called him—and I was a liar and a tramp and God was punishing me. No one had ever talked that way around my house. I'd never even heard the word *whore* before—until my mother called me one. Isn't that funny?

"Do you know what it's like?" she asks, turning to me. "Do you know what it's like to have your family turn you out of their house and tell you you aren't their daughter?

They told me to leave and never come back. It feels like I died. That's what they wanted. They wanted me to die, but I was still alive. Do you know how that feels?"

I know how it feels to want to die. But I don't know what it's like to have your family turn you out like that. I tell Cheryl no, I have no idea how that feels.

Late Friday I wake up in the middle of the night and feel something funny. I'm wet between my legs. I pull down my panties and see I've been bleeding. It scares me to death. I lie there until dawn, trying not to move.

I'm lying on my back, as usual. I haven't slept on my stomach in months. My stomach rises up from my body and makes me think of the flat-topped mountains they have in west Texas. They call them mesas because they look like tables. Every day my skin is stretched tighter and tighter over my stomach, and it hurts. I don't have a regular belly button any long. It pokes out now instead of in, and it feels as soft as a baby's skin.

A baby's. I feel the baby move every day. I can even see it move these days. I can lie and watch my stomach and see—what? An elbow or a foot or a head? It's hard to tell. But it moves around and sometimes it jabs me in the ribs. Other times the baby has the hiccups. I feel it twitch again and again in a funny kind of rhythm. After a while it stops, and I wonder if the baby's sleeping. It would be all curled up, like the pictures I've seen in Thomas's office. Maybe it's sucking its thumb.

I feel between my legs, but I can't find any more

blood. I wonder what will happen if I stand up. Will I bleed more? Will I lose the baby?

I think of the baby sleeping inside me. What if it dies? It will be my fault. I've wanted it to die so many times. I've thought about hot baths, throwing myself down stairs, doing anything so I wouldn't have the baby—and my life could go on.

But I feel different now. I want to keep the baby inside me. I want to feel it move and know it's safe. I'll lie here forever if I have to. I won't move if it's dangerous for the baby.

I may have an incompetent cervix. Harriet told Cheryl and me about women who have problems like that. "You know what an incompetent cervix is?" she said. We didn't. "It means everything could be going along just fine and then the woman stands up and her baby falls out on the ground—just like that. Fortunately that will never happen to me," she told us. "All the babies in my family were overdue by about two or three months. The women in my family have extremely competent cervixes."

I realize Harriet probably didn't know what she was talking about as usual, but I don't want to take any chances. My cervix may be very incompetent. So I don't even get up to go to the bathroom, which is beginning to kill me. I doze off and on.

When I can see the clock says eight, I get up slowly and carefully. Nothing happens. The baby doesn't fall out on the floor, and I'm not bleeding any longer. I get dressed and go to see Thomas. He's always here by eight on Saturday mornings.

Thomas makes me sit down when I get to his office, and he listens to the baby's heartbeat. "It sounds fine," he says reassuringly.

Then he asks me to put my feet in the stirrups. I hate that. It always makes me feel like a turkey getting stuffed at Thanksgiving. But I know I have to do it. Thomas wouldn't make me put my feet in the stirrups if it wasn't absolutely necessary.

I want him to be with me when my baby's born. Maybe he'll hold my hand when the pains get bad. It won't hurt as much if he's there with me.

Finally Thomas is finished. He gives me his hand and helps me sit up again.

"Everything's fine," he says. "The baby's heartbeat is steady. You may have bled a little—but not enough to hurt you or the baby. You shouldn't do much for the rest of the day, but you don't need to worry, Anne."

Thomas looks at me steadily while he talks with those beautiful blue-green eyes. That's what I like about him. He treats me like an adult. He respects me.

I watch him out of the corner of my eye when I leave the office. He's bent over a clipboard, writing something. He's so dedicated. All he cares about is his patients.

Thomas doesn't wear a wedding ring, I think as I walk down the hall. He probably doesn't have a personal life since he's so dedicated to his work. He must be lonely, even if he doesn't realize it. I wonder what he does at night when he's all by himself.

The Eleventh Week
October 29–November 4

Someone bangs on our door on Sunday morning at three. It's Nancy. She sticks her head inside and hisses at us.

"Gracie's in labor," she says, and motions for us to come.

Cheryl and I pull on our robes and wander out into the hall. It's dark, and all you can see is a pale stripe of light from Gracie and Nancy's room. We knock softly and go inside.

Gracie is lying there in bed. She has her knees up, making a small tent out of the blanket. She looks like she's ten years old, and I wonder again how she'll ever manage to have a baby.

Nancy bursts through the door. She's carrying a damp washcloth, which she puts on Gracie's forehead. Gracie doesn't say anything. She just lies there and stares at all of us with her wide, hazel eyes. She looks scared to death.

"She's having contractions every seven minutes now," Nancy says. "I've been timing them for an hour. She's not due till Thanksgiving, but the doctor told her that young girls often have premature babies. Maybe it's better that way," she tells Cheryl and me in a softer voice. "She'll have a smaller baby at least."

Cheryl and I sit on Nancy's bed. I'm not sure what we're doing here. We don't know Gracie that well. Nobody knows Gracie that well. She almost never says anything, and she never looks anyone in the eye. When she walks, she doesn't make any noise. She just slips along the walls like a mouse and disappears.

She's whimpering now. She starts to breathe harder and harder, and her eyes widen and she looks panicky. She must be having a contraction. Nancy grabs her hand and holds it.

I'm glad Nancy's doing something. I have no idea what to do. I don't want to watch someone in so much pain, especially someone who's so young and scared. But I know I can't leave. I'm part of this now, I realize. It surprises me, but I know it's true. I can't look at any of this from a distance, the way I wanted to. I don't know how it happened, but I know I need to be here.

"She's having contractions every five minutes now," Nancy announces, looking at her watch. "You need to go wake Mrs. Marshall, Anne."

I'm still sleepy, and it takes me a minute to figure out what she's talking about. That's right, I think. Mrs. Landing's out of town for the weekend. I can't believe she picked this weekend to go out of town. Gracie's in labor, and we need her here.

Some woman named Mrs. Marshall is taking Mrs. Landing's place. We don't know Mrs. Marshall that well, and I don't think we can trust her. She has pale, fidgety eyes and sparse gray hair, and I think that's a sign her family's been inbreeding for generations. She's probably her own grandmother. I can't imagine what she'll do when she hears someone's in labor. She'll probably disappear and we'll find her hiding in the freezer three days later. By then, Gracie and her baby will both be dead.

I run down the hall and pound on Mrs. Marshall's door. I hear a noise inside, so I pound again. Maybe Mrs. Marshall is trying to make a getaway out the window.

Finally she opens the door. Her hair's in brush rollers that are falling out, and she's frantically trying to roll them back up and stick pins in them.

"Is something wrong?" she asks.

"Gracie's in labor," I tell her, "and we need to get her to the hospital. Her contractions are only five minutes apart."

Mrs. Marshall stares at me, still trying to pin up her hair. Doesn't she understand? Gracie's going to die if we don't hurry. "We have to get Gracie to the hospital as soon as we can," I repeat. "She's too small to have a baby. We need to leave now."

"I'll get dressed." Mrs. Marshall closes the door.

She manages to get dressed, but it takes her fifteen minutes. By then, Gracie's screaming and crying, and everyone else is awake. Gracie's face is so pale that every freckle stands out on her cheeks.

"I never thought it would hurt this much," she says. "They never said it would hurt like this." Her face crumples and she screams again. Tears run down her cheeks.

"We'd better get her out to the car," Mrs. Marshall says. I can tell immediately that she doesn't include herself in the "we." She's about as smart as a doorstop, but she isn't nearly as useful. I can't believe Mrs. Landing left her with us. We might as well be by ourselves.

Cheryl and Nancy help Gracie to her feet. She walks a few steps, then doubles over. They pick her up and carry her. She's so light, they don't have to strain.

Mrs. Marshall and I follow along. She has her purse clutched to her waist. "I've got the car keys here," she says to no one in particular. "I always keep them with me."

The home's car is a blue Chevy station wagon, and the backseat is down. We spread a blanket over it and help Gracie get in.

Mrs. Marshall flutters around like a big, stupid bird. "Is this a stick shift?" she asks, peering into the driver's seat. "I never learned how to drive a stick shift." She jangles the keys like they're castanets. She can't do anything, I realize. She can't help us at all.

"I'll drive," I say. I reach over and grab the car keys.

I slide in under the steering wheel with about an inch to spare. I haven't driven in months, and the seating's a lot tighter than it used to be. But I love to drive. It makes me feel free, and it reminds me I'm competent at one thing at least. I ram the car into gear and we roar off.

"Not so fast," Mrs. Marshall gasps, over and over. Every time I hear her, I push the gas pedal farther down.

The trees and bushes whip past, and the night air pours in through the windows. Gracie screams sometimes and other times, she whimpers. What if she has the baby in the car? They'll both die. I know women don't die in childbirth these days, but Gracie isn't a woman. She's a kid. She's so small, she could die more easily. We have to hurry. I press the gas pedal harder.

"Not so fast," Mrs. Marshall repeats.

"Shut up!" I hear someone say. It's Nancy. Good for her. Mrs. Marshall doesn't open her mouth for the rest of the drive.

It's ten miles to the hospital, and we get there in seven minutes. I'm proud of that. We screech through the parking lot to the emergency entrance. I hit the horn and it blares and echoes in the hospital carport.

The same two hospital workers who came for LaNelle wander outside, rubbing their eyes. They don't look any smarter or more competent than the last time I saw them. They pull a stretcher to the car, and Nancy and I jump out to unlock the rear door. Gracie is lying there in a small heap.

One of the two idiots looks at her strangely. "She looks mighty young t'be havin' a baby," he says.

"You want to check her ID or something?" Nancy snaps. "She's not here to buy a drink. Shut up and get her into that hospital."

You can tell they're used to being bossed around, because they don't say anything more. They manage to lift Gracie onto the stretcher without dropping her, which is a miracle.

The rest of us stand outside the car and watch as they roll her through the doors and disappear. It's still dark outside, and suddenly it feels cold, too. I dressed quickly and I forgot to put on a sweater. I rub my hands up and down my arms to try to warm myself.

"Do you think we should go inside?" Cheryl asks.

Nancy shakes her head. "Uh-uh," she says. "We wouldn't be able to stay with her anyway. Let's go get some coffee and doughnuts. I saw a place close to here that's already open."

We get back in the car and drive off. None of us say anything to Mrs. Marshall, who's staring out the window and sulking. Every minute or two she heaves a big sigh to let us know how aggrieved she is.

Ike's Coffee Shop is a few blocks away. You can probably see it for miles, since it's the only place in town that's lit up. It's made out of old cement blocks that have been painted white with green trim. The paint is peeling and the awnings are drooping, and you have to lower your head to walk through the door if you're any taller than a dwarf.

Inside, it's all cracked linoleum and bad wallpaper, and the windows are fogged up from the heat of the stove. Bacon and eggs are crackling in a frying pan, and they smell greasy but good. There are only a few people at the counter and booths, and they're crouched over newspapers, drinking steaming coffee to wake themselves up. No one pays much attention to us.

Nancy and Cheryl and I sit at one of the red vinyl booths and order coffee and glazed doughnuts. I've never drunk coffee, but it seems like a good time to start. I pour a bunch of milk and sugar into it. It isn't too bad. We sit and stir our coffee around and polish off a dozen doughnuts. I haven't eaten this much in months. It's wonderful to eat something that isn't good for me. I've forgotten how much I love junk food.

Mrs. Marshall sits by herself at the counter. She's ignoring us. She seems to know all the other customers, the waitresses, and the cook. They may be her relatives, since they all look as dim-witted as she does.

The sky's beginning to get lighter. More customers come in, dressed in cowboy hats and boots. One of the waitresses, whose hair is the same shade as a yellow crayon, greets them all familiarly and jokes with them.

"My mother works in a place like this in Jackson," Nancy says. "She's been there forever, like that waitress."

That's a funny thing for her to say. For some reason I thought Nancy was from a family with money. Maybe I assumed that because of all her talk about her sorority and college. I can't imagine having a mother who works in a restaurant like this. I can't imagine my mother lifting a finger anywhere. She hasn't in years.

"Are you close to her?" Cheryl asks. She's always interested in other girls' parents. I think it's because her own family is a bunch of creeps.

Nancy shrugs and drinks her coffee. "I guess so," she says noncommittally. "My goal in life is not to be like her. Does that mean I'm close to her?"

For a minute she looks sad. But maybe it's my imagination. "You meet a lot of men working in a place like this," Nancy says. "Mom's spent her life trying to find the perfect man. She married two of them, and the rest came and went. I always knew when another one had left. I'd hear her crying late at night, and I'd find empty liquor bottles in the trash the next morning."

She stares into her coffee cup and grins halfheartedly. "But it'd always be all right eventually," she says. "A new man always came along. And then she'd be happy again, sometimes for months."

Nancy swigs her coffee, then stands up abruptly. She grabs her purse and walks to the jukebox. A few minutes later she's back. "I'm playing 'Your Cheatin' Heart' three times," she says. "Y'all know anyone you want to dedicate it to?"

The sounds of a steel guitar twang in the background. I hate country-and-western music. My father thinks the whole point of country music is self-pity. He says that's fine if you like that kind of thing, but he doesn't think self-pity is an art form.

Maybe that kind of music reminds Nancy of her mother, though. The whole idea of an aging waitress and an endless stream of men and heartbreak and alcohol sounds exactly like a bad country-and-western song to me. One of those awful woman singers with big hair and long fingernails could make a million dollars singing it. It would sell out in all the trailer parks across the country.

Nancy is quiet right now, listening to the music. It's the first time I can remember her being this quiet. If I had a mother like hers, I'd be quiet too. I might even listen to country-and-western music.

"So what do you all think of Dr. Blanchard?" I ask casually. "Has anybody heard whether he's married?"

Nancy looks at me and cocks an eyebrow. "I doubt it," she says. "He's queer, you know."

What does she mean? She must be confused. "I'm talking about Dr. Blanchard," I point out patiently. "Thomas Blanchard, our doctor at the home."

Nancy starts to laugh. "Oh, God, Anne. You poor thing. You're almost as naive as Rachel. Everybody knows he's queer. He lives in town with some high school teacher—some *male* high school teacher. And his name isn't Thomas. It's Melvin, for God's sake."

I stir my coffee and watch it swirl around. I must have stirred it too hard, because it spills over the edge of the cup. "I don't think you know what you're talking about."

Nancy has spent most of her life in dumps like this, I think. She doesn't understand a man like Thomas. Just because he doesn't go around belching and chewing tobacco and scratching his crotch, Nancy automatically thinks he's a homosexual. That's what happens when you come from a lower-class background. Nancy doesn't have much refinement. That's her problem.

"Trust me, Anne," Nancy says. "I know what I'm talking about."

When I glance at her, she isn't laughing anymore. She

looks like she feels sorry for me. I hate it when people feel sorry for me. Especially people who don't have any refinement.

The three of us sit at the booth for a little longer, until the sun is up. Before we leave town, we drive by the hospital and go in. A receptionist is behind the front desk. She's tall and thin, like a female Ichabod Crane. She stares at us in a cold, nasty way when we ask about Gracie.

"You're not relatives, are you?" she says. She knows we aren't. She knows we're from the home.

When we shake our heads, she smiles at us. I've handled ice that's warmer than her smile. "I'm afraid I can't give out any information on one of our patients to someone who isn't a relative," she says.

The three of us stare at her for a minute. She stares straight back at us, mean and cold and arrogant. Finally we turn and shuffle off. "Bitch," Nancy mutters.

I wonder if the receptionist would treat Mrs. Marshall better. Probably. Probably she'd be nicer to anyone than to three unwed pregnant girls from the home. If there's a God, that receptionist will develop an incurable disease in the next three minutes. It's too bad I don't believe in God.

Mrs. Marshall is in the car by herself. She's still miffed about Nancy's telling her to shut up.

"I intend to have a very serious talk with Mrs. Landing when she gets back," she says as we drive out of town. "I may never return to the home after this."

She's waiting for all of us to apologize and beg her to

reconsider. When that doesn't happen, she finally shuts up. She goes back to sighing every few seconds until we get back to the home.

We don't hear anything about Gracie until noon on Monday. By then Mrs. Landing is back, and Mrs. Marshall has already left in a huff. We're sitting at the dining table eating when Mrs. Landing comes in and sits down with us.

"I thought you'd all like to know about Gracie," she says. "The doctor had to give her a caesarean section. Gracie was too small to give birth—even though her baby only weighed five pounds."

I wonder if a caesarean hurts as much as labor. If it doesn't hurt as much, then I want one. I doubt they give you a choice, though. Not at that country hospital, anyway.

I heard a rumor that the doctors and nurses at that hospital don't give as many painkillers to girls from the home. They don't like us. They think it's good for us to suffer a little. I've forgotten who I heard that from. Maybe it's one of those dumb rumors I'm always hearing that isn't true.

After meeting that hospital receptionist, though, I'm not sure. I can see her watching us with that hateful, superior smile. She wouldn't care if we died having our babies. She'd enjoy it. Maybe they have a quota to meet at that hospital—maybe one of the girls from the home has to die every year. It would be great material for the local preachers. The news would go as far as Oklahoma, where Pastor Browning could scream hellfire and damnation about it. (It sounds just like *The Scarlet Letter* to me. I wonder if Cheryl's read it. Probably not, I decide. I bet they don't allow books like that in Oklahoma. They'd think it's about Communism, just like *The Red Badge of Courage*.)

Gracie had a baby boy, Mrs. Landing says. The baby is small, but he's healthy. Gracie is all right too. She's been sleeping off and on since the surgery.

"I'm sorry I wasn't here when Gracie went into labor," Mrs. Landing says. "But it sounds as if all of you handled it quite well. You were able to take care of yourselves and Gracie too—without me here. Thank you."

She doesn't say anything about Mrs. Marshall and how rudely we treated her. As a matter of fact, we never see Mrs. Marshall again.

Our group topic hits a new low on Tuesday. Abortion, for God's sake. It's all I can do not to roll my eyes when Mrs. Landing announces it. Here we are, about to start delivering babies pretty soon. We might as well talk about Kotex or PMS as long as we're at it.

"Isn't abortion a little beside the point right now?" I ask. "Shouldn't we be talking about more important things?"

I'm talking in these meetings now. It's a big breakthrough. Maybe if I start talking more, I won't be so sneaky and passive-aggressive. That way I can develop a new, better personality.

"I think it's something you need to talk about, Anne," Mrs. Landing says. "Somewhere along the line all of you made a decision not to have an abortion. Why? Why did you choose to go ahead and have your babies and give them up?"

Harriet raises her hand. She's the only one who ever raises her hand in those groups. She seems to think she's still in school. She looks like she knows the right answer and she wants the teacher to call on her so she can show everybody how smart she is. She's waving her pipe-cleaner arm like she's in a big room full of people— instead of just seven of us. I hope she has a best friend who'll tell her she needs to use a stronger deodorant. I'm going to have to start wearing clothespins on my nose at these meetings.

"I never even considered an abortion," Harriet says. "I don't know how anybody could. It's against the Lord's will."

Once Harriet starts talking like that, she won't stop. It's like a coughing fit. She yaks on and on about the sanctity of life and how the baby she's carrying is very precious to the Lord because it's an innocent life.

"I'm just grateful I had parents that taught me right from wrong," she says, "and that I've accepted the Lord into my life."

Oh, brother. I wonder when Harriet's going to wise up and figure out the facts of life. If my toilet-seat hypothesis isn't correct, she took a quick roll in the hay and she accepted a lot more than the Lord into her life. I can see Harriet lying there, thinking, Boy! The Lord really *does* move in mysterious ways!

It kills me because Harriet always seems to be so sure

about everything. It must be nice to go through life thinking you have all the answers and dying to tell everybody about them. Harriet spends most of her days looking so smug, I want to hit her. I keep hoping that she'll read a book about saints and decide to become a martyr and throw herself on a pitchfork instead of torturing us to death by preaching all the time.

Nancy looks as irritated as I am. She still carries a grudge about Harriet's turning us in for drinking. She told us she studied about people like Harriet in freshman psychology at Ole Miss. They called them paranoid schizophrenics, except she didn't think Harriet was as smart as most schizophrenics. If she were smarter, she'd be getting messages from people like Marie Antoinette or Robert E. Lee instead of God. Hearing messages from God isn't all that original.

"I think you're saying the most ignorant garbage I've ever heard in my life," Nancy tells Harriet. "I've known a few girls who've had abortions, and there's no way on earth I'd get one. I knew someone who almost bled to death after an abortion. And another girl who'll never be able to have children because they botched it so badly. God doesn't have anything to do with it. It's dangerous, and I'd never risk my life that way."

Harriet looks mad, but she has a thin smile on her face. "I'll pray for you, Nancy," she says.

"Don't bother," Nancy says. "I can pray for myself."

I can tell Harriet can hardly wait to get away so she can go talk to the Lord about Nancy and arrange for her to drop dead this afternoon. I'm waiting for Rachel to jump in and give us Bob Dylan's views on abortion, but she doesn't. She sits there, staring at her lap. She's seemed different the past few days—quieter. Sometimes she looks like she's been crying.

I don't say anything more, because I don't know what I think. I've never known anyone who had an abortion. All I know is that it's dangerous and it seems dirty, somehow. My mother and I never talked about abortion. Dr. Lawrence, our doctor in Dallas, never mentioned it either.

The only choice I had was to come here and have the baby. Then I'd leave, and it would all be over. At the time, it was simple and clear.

All my letters continue to pile up. They make a nice, tidy bundle in my drawer. Sometimes I think I'll let the bundle get bigger and bigger and then I'll set it on fire. I wonder what those letters will smell like when they burn.

Tigress, from Pamela's letters. She must be sick of it, because she poured it all over her letters to me. She probably has some new, hot perfume that's making her irresistible.

Pity, from my mother's letters. I'm not sure what pity smells like when you set it on fire. I'm sure it's one of those smells that lingers, though.

And what about my father's letters? I'm not sure there would be any smell from them. They're clean and cold and bloodless. Burn them, and they'll disappear without a trace. They won't even leave ashes behind.

I think a lot about my father. I wonder if he ever thinks about me. Looking back, I realize that his feelings were always temporary. I never thought he loved my mother as much after she had her breakdown. She failed him, and that meant she wasn't the person he thought she was.

Daddy and I got closer when Mother was in the hospital. That seemed nice to me at the time. I was the solid one, the one Daddy could depend on. But now I wonder about it. Didn't he just transfer his love to me because my mother didn't deserve it? And now I don't deserve his love either, so he moves on somewhere else. I haven't been the person he wants me to be. How could he love someone who disappointed him? He couldn't.

It's funny. I thought I had a huge stockpile with my father. I thought he'd always love me. All those straight A's, all those remarks from my teachers about how smart I was, all my plans for college and my future. Daddy was so proud of me!

I heard him brag to other people about me. When I heard him talk, I felt wonderful. It was proof of how much he loved me. I noticed it made my mother angry when Daddy bragged about me so much, and that made me feel strange. I'd read enough books to realize mothers could be jealous of their daughters, and I thought that was the problem. I didn't want my mother to be jealous of me, but I didn't know what to say. All I knew was I was making her angrier and angrier, no matter what I said.

Maybe that's why Mother isn't angry at me any longer.

She doesn't have any reason to be jealous of me. My father doesn't love me now.

I don't know what it's like to be turned out of my own house. But I know what it's like to disappear. That's what happened to me with my father.

I told him I was pregnant in July. I waited and waited, till I was sure. I'd been sick to my stomach for a few days, and my father came to my room one night to see how I was. I knew I had to tell him. I didn't want to hurt him, but I knew he was the one I had to tell. There wasn't anyone else.

I practiced the words over and over in my mind, and I knew I was trying to convince myself they were true. "Daddy, I have to tell you something. I'm pregnant." When those words finally came out, it seemed like someone else said them. They stayed there in the air and they echoed, because there wasn't another sound.

I closed my eyes. I didn't want to see my father hurt. I hated to see him hurt. But then I opened my eyes, and I didn't see that. All I saw was this funny look on his face. Daddy didn't look sad or hurt or angry or anything. He didn't look like anything at all. He just stared at me for a few seconds, and then he walked out and closed the door. He never said anything.

A few minutes later the door opened and my mother came in. I looked at her face and I saw everything—anger and satisfaction and sadness and pity and something else I couldn't recognize. She looked completely alive for the first time in years.

"It's time for us to talk," she said. "Just the two of us. Your father's not going to have anything to do with this."

At our group meeting on Friday, Rachel proposes the topic she wants us to discuss.

"Equality of men and women," she says. "You might not have heard of it around here. But it's a big issue in California."

This is the first time Rachel's talked in days. She's been staying in her room and playing records for hours. When she showed up in the dining room, she pushed her food around on the plate and didn't eat it.

"Worried about your weight, Rachel?" Nancy asked her one night. "Maybe you've been around me too much. You're getting as vain as I am." She grinned and waited for Rachel to take the bait and tell her how unenlightened she was.

But Rachel didn't say anything. She stared down at her plate and shrugged.

Later on, in the middle of the night, I was walking down the hall on my way back from the bathroom. I heard the sound of someone crying. It got louder and I finally realized it was coming from Rachel's room. She still doesn't have a roommate, and I knew it had to be her crying.

I stood in front of her door for a long time. I couldn't decide what to do. Maybe Rachel wanted to be alone, and she'd hate it if someone heard her crying and wanted to come in and talk to her. That's the way I used to feel. I didn't want anyone around, ever.

Maybe it would help Rachel if she talked to me, though. I know what it's like to feel terrible and hopeless. I feel like that most of the time.

But what if Rachel was crying about politics or Vietnam or something equally boring? I wouldn't know what to say, since I didn't think politics was worth crying about. To cheer her up, I'd have to say I was planning to become a Communist and I wanted her advice about how to overthrow the government. (Maybe that wouldn't be so bad, being a Communist. It might be better than being a nun.)

I was still standing there, trying to decide what to do, when the crying stopped. Everything was quiet. I stood there for a few more minutes, then I went back to my room. When I saw Rachel the next morning, her eyes were red. She looked sadder than I'd ever seen her look, and I wondered if I'd made the right decision.

But right now, for the first time in days she seems like the old Rachel. She shakes back her long, frizzy hair from her face and starts to talk. "Haven't any of you noticed any problems?" she asks. "Women don't earn as much as men. We don't have the same job opportunities. We're second-class citizens, and most of us don't even notice. We're so used to it, we don't even see it.

"If you want an example of how unequal things are, just look at you," she goes on. She's getting more and more worked up now. "You're here for three or four months, stuck away because your families are ashamed of you. You're going to have to go through childbirth by yourselves. Well, what about the guys who got you pregnant? They haven't suffered at all. There's not a damn thing that's fair about that."

"So what?" Nancy says. "You can keep blabbing till the cows come home, and it won't change anything. Women still get pregnant and men still don't. That's true, whether you like it or not. It's even true in an insane asylum like California."

Then Harriet has to put in her two cents about what the Bible says. "It's all there," she says, waving her spindly arm in the air. "It's all in the Bible. Men and women are different. Our roles are different. It's God's will. Do you remember Genesis? Eve led Adam into temptation."

I've had enough out of Harriet and Adam and Eve and Genesis and every other book in the whole damn Bible. "I don't know about you, Harriet," I say. "But in my case, it was Adam who was doing all the leading into temptation. And the goddamn apple wasn't even worth it."

I can't believe I actually said the word *goddamn* in a meeting. But it seems appropriate under the circumstances. Harriet looks as if I slapped her, which isn't a bad idea.

Cheryl backs me up for some reason. "I met one of those Adams myself," she says. "And Anne's right about the apple. The one I got was bad too."

She and I start to laugh. Rachel looks quite pleased at all the participation.

"Imagine what it would be like," she announces dramatically, "if men and women were equal. We could have babies if we weren't married and we wouldn't have to give them up to strangers. We could live by ourselves and work and be free."

Rachael goes on talking about men and women and freedom and babies, and all those other ideas that get her excited. I watch her carefully, and I wonder again if she believes what she's saying. Today she's acting the way she used to—talking a lot and telling us how everything's getting better. But there's something different about her, something sad, that I don't understand. All I know is it's making me feel worse and worse to listen to her.

I look at my stomach, which is rising up to greet me. I think of Jake. He's in school now, carefree and perfectly happy. He hasn't suffered at all. He doesn't even know about the baby—I made certain of that. His life has gone on, uninterrupted, and mine has stopped. Of course it's unfair and hateful and disgusting. I've always known that. I don't need Rachel to tell me.

But knowing it doesn't change anything. Life's unfair—so what? The world isn't changing or getting better for us. Rachel's crazy if she thinks she can change things, and she's going to be terribly disappointed. She doesn't understand that it's so much better to look at life the way it is.

A few years ago I found my mother crying, and I asked her what was wrong. "Being a woman is horrible," she said. "You'll find that out someday. You and Pamela will both find that out."

Later my mother came to my room and said she'd been upset. I shouldn't pay any attention to her—she hadn't meant what she said.

But I knew she had. When my mother talked in a quiet voice, I learned never to believe what she said. It was only when she was crying or screaming that she managed to tell the truth.

"Being a woman is horrible." I think about that sometimes when I'm feeling bad. It's horrible, and it's not getting any better, either. I look at Rachel and wonder when she's going to realize that.

The Twelfth Week
November 5-11

On Sunday, Cheryl, Nancy, Rachel, and I go to visit Gracie in the hospital. She's on the second floor, in the maternity ward.

We walk along the hall, and I can't help looking in the other rooms. It seems like every one has mothers and babies in them. Their rooms are filled with brightly colored flowers that make the air smell heavy and sweet, and the women look happy and excited. Once or twice we hear a baby cry.

Gracie has a single room at the end of the hall. She smiles when we come in, but she looks as if she's been crying. She's thin and pale, and she has dark circles under her eyes.

"You're my first visitors," she says, "except for Mrs. Landing."

We sit on the edges of chairs and tables and try to

make some kind of cheerful conversation. It's hard. We don't have much to talk about that's cheerful.

After a few minutes the conversation dwindles. Gracie is looking down.

"It was nice of you to come and see me," she says. "I've been so lonely here. I hadn't thought I could be any lonelier than I was at the home—but I have been. I've missed all of you."

Her eyes fill with tears, and Nancy pats her hand. Gracie looks up and tries to smile at us. All of a sudden I realize that she thinks of us as friends. Who knows? Maybe we're the only friends she has. It makes me feel terrible to think that, and I hope it isn't true. I look around her bare little room, and I think about how happy and bright and noisy the other mothers' rooms were.

"Have you seen your baby?" Cheryl asks.

Gracie shakes her head. "I couldn't," she says. "The nurses told me it was better that way. Since they had to put me to sleep for the caesarean, I never saw him at all. Sometimes I walk along the halls, and I look at the babies. And I wonder if I'd be able to recognize him. It seems like I should know him, doesn't it? Don't you think a mother recognizes her baby even if she's never seen him?"

She starts to cry softly. "But I've signed the papers," she says. "The social worker told me that was the right thing to do. She told me I had to be strong for my baby. She promised me he'd go to good parents—wonderful parents, she said—who could give him everything I couldn't. She told me I was doing the right thing," Gracie repeats. "She was right, wasn't she?"

"Of course she was right," Nancy says. She's still patting Gracie's hand. "You didn't have any other choice. You can't think about it anymore."

I can't stay here any longer. I can't look at Gracie, and I can't listen to her story. I have to leave. I say something about needing a glass of water, and I wander into the hall.

The babies have all been returned to the nursery, and the curtains are open so you can see them. There are two rows of them—mostly bald and red faced and tiny. I try not to look too closely.

But I have to walk past a small group of people who are crowded outside the nursery, craning their necks and taking pictures with bright, popping flashbulbs. There are children, looking at tiny brothers and sisters, and proud grandparents, and new fathers with wide happy grins. They're laughing and calling out to each other and trying to get their babies to look at them.

I try not to listen to them, but I can't help it. I walk past the nurses' station and take the first exit staircase I find.

According to Thomas, my due date is sometime in December. That's a few weeks from now. I'm beginning to wish it wasn't so close.

Something strange has happened to me. I don't want to leave the home. I want to stay, because I feel safe here. I'm safe and my baby's safe.

I don't want to stop being pregnant, either. I can't believe I'm saying that, but it's true. There's something so nice and secure about wrapping my arms around my stomach and feeling the baby move. It makes me think that when you're pregnant, you're never alone and you're never lonely. You always have someone with you.

The baby's gotten so big. I can look at my stomach and watch him move. He jabs me sometimes, with an elbow or a knee. He's a part of me right now. But then I'll give birth, and they'll take him away from me. Maybe I'll never see him or hear him cry. Maybe he'll disappear when I'm asleep, the way Gracie's baby did. I'll spend the rest of my life wondering what he looks like.

I used to think pregnancy and giving up a baby were some kind of punishment I'd earned for being foolish and weak. I don't believe that now. I can't believe that any of us—me or Cheryl or Rachel or Nancy or Gracie or even Harriet—deserve this kind of punishment. I think of giving up my baby, and it feels like a knife slashing through my body and killing me inside. No one deserves that kind of punishment. No one.

I know I'm stupid and slow about things. But I actually expected that staying here would be the worst part. I had to get through the next four months, and then I'd be all right. I believed that! I believed it was something I had to get through, like a door or window, and then, like magic, I'd be my old self again.

I don't know what I've gotten myself into and I don't know how to get out. Some nights I feel panicky. I'm scared to death of childbirth and all the pain, but I know that's not going to be the worst part. I'll have to sign papers, like Gracie did, saying that I'm giving up the baby. I'm supposed to carry him for months and then give him up. Forget it ever happened and go back to my old life.

I'm crying a lot these days. I've never cried like this before. Sometimes it seems like I could cry forever and never stop and never use up all my tears. After I finish crying, I don't feel better. I feel dead inside.

At night it's even worse. Sometimes I dream about a child who's lost. He has a sad, scared look on his face and I want to help him, but I can't. I see him, then he disappears. I try to find him. I run up and down a hallway full of doors and look in and try to find him. He isn't there. He's gone. All I can feel is an ache and dread and panic that spread all over me and cover my face and my heart and press down on me. When I feel that, I know that he's gone forever and I'll never see him again.

I wake up crying from those dreams, and then I can't get back to sleep. Sometimes I don't want to sleep anyway, because I'm scared I'll have that dream again. I'd rather never sleep again than have that dream.

I'm feeling so bad about all of this that I go to see Mrs. Landing. It's the first time I've talked to her in a long time. Every time I start to talk, I cry. Then I try to talk again. That embarrasses me. I hate to cry in front of people. I feel like a mess most of the time—but at least I keep it to myself. This time, I can't.

But I have to say that Mrs. Landing is very nice and patient with me. She seems to understand everything I'm saying, even when I'm sobbing or blowing my nose or wiping my face.

"What you're going through is perfectly normal, Anne," she says. "It's a terrible thing to have to give up your baby. Most people have no idea how terrible it is."

I sit here in her office for a long time and listen to her talk. Finally I stop crying. I feel empty and used up.

"Does it ever get better?" I ask her.

She shakes her head, just a little. "They say you'll forget all of this someday," she says.

When I look at her closely, I realize she doesn't believe that any more than I do.

Tuesday afternoon Rachel comes in our room and closes the door. This place is like Grand Central Station. Nancy is already in here, sitting on Cheryl's bed and hogging all the space and lecturing us about men. She thinks Cheryl and I need lots of advice.

Rachel doesn't say anything. She just closes the door and starts sinking onto the floor right in front of it. It's hard to carry on a conversation with Rachel sinking on the floor. She has on a bright red caftan and her hair is even frizzier than usual. She has a funny, wild expression in her eyes.

Nancy looks irritated. She's been talking to us about flirting and how she's great at it and it's practically what she's majoring in at college. She hates to be interrupted when she's talking about herself.

"Do you have something you want to tell us, Rachel?" she says.

Rachel doesn't say anything for a minute. Then she closes her eyes and lets out a breath. "David just called me," she says.

"David?" Cheryl echoes. "Is he your boyfriend?"

Rachel nods. "He wants us to get married and keep the baby."

She puts her head in her lap. She's crying. I've heard Rachel cry before, that night when I was standing outside her room. But I've never seen her cry, and there's something terrible and lonely about it. I can feel tears in my eyes, even though I don't know why she's crying.

Rachel yanks up her head and starts talking again. "Goddammit," she says. "Goddammit to hell. That's what I wanted him to say for so long. Why did he have to wait so damn long?"

She puts her head back in her lap and begins to cry again. I stare at Cheryl and Nancy. They look as blank as I do. Cheryl gets up and walks over to Rachel. She sits down on the floor next to her and strokes her hair.

"It's all right," Cheryl says. "It's all right." I don't know why she's saying that. I still don't know what's wrong.

Rachel stops crying after a few minutes. She raises up her head again. Her face is blotchy and tear-stained. She starts talking again in a tired, dull voice.

"He was the only man I ever slept with," she says. "He knew he was the first. I was in love with him, and he knew that, too. I thought he loved me. I actually thought he loved me.

"But then I got pregnant. You know what he said to me when I told him? He asked me if I was sure he was the father. I couldn't believe he'd say something like that. He acted like it was all my fault, too. Like I'd gotten pregnant by myself. He asked me what I was going to do about it. He acted like it was my problem and not his."

She pulls her hair back from her face. Some of it sticks where her face is wet and she brushes it back, trying to smooth it. "That bastard," she says. "That damned bastard. Him and my goddamn parents, all three of them. Goddamn them."

Nancy shrugs. "You wanted to get married and keep the baby," she says. "And now he wants to get married. So what's the problem? So what if it took him a little while? Men are kind of slow sometimes."

"You don't understand a goddamn thing," Rachel says. "Yeah, this is what I wanted. But I don't have the faintest frigging idea what I want anymore. Everything seems so different now." She starts to cry again. "I don't know what I want," she repeats.

David called her, I think slowly. David called and wants to marry Rachel. Maybe he acted like a bastard once. But he wants to marry her now. He must love her.

I know Rachel's feeling terrible, but for a few minutes I envy her so much that I feel like I've been kicked in the stomach. It hurts to breathe. I wonder what it's like, to have someone love you and want to marry you. I try to imagine Jake calling me. He never told me he loved me, and I can't think of him saying those words. I love you. I want to marry you. I want to spend my life with you. No matter how hard I try, I can't imagine it.

For about an hour Rachel and Nancy stay in our room and talk. They go back and forth, with Rachel saying things like how she hates men and Nancy telling her not to make such a big deal of it.

"Especially if David's rich," Nancy says. "Is he rich, by the way?" She's speaking very casually, but I can tell she's dying to find out.

Rachel ignores her. "Maybe I'll just go back to California and become a lesbian," she says loudly. "I think I'm through with men."

"My God." Nancy looks horrified. "Shut your mouth, Rachel. Do you know what you're saying? If you're a lesbian, you have to be around women all the time, for the rest of your life. It's even worse than a sorority. I don't know how anybody stands it."

Rachel appears unimpressed. She's stopped listening to the rest of us anyway. Finally she gets up and leaves. "I need to be alone now," she says. "I'm going to my room."

She stays in her room the rest of the afternoon. Cheryl goes to talk to her and comes back a few minutes later, looking puzzled.

"Now Rachel's acting even stranger," she says. "She's in her room listening to the same album over and over— *Sergeant Pepper's Lonely Hearts Club Band,* instead of Bob Dylan. She says she's waiting to hear the answer from it because it's a mystical album."

"Good God," Nancy says. She's still in our room,

thumbing through fashion magazines. It's important to keep up with the styles, even if we can't wear them right now, she's told us.

"If Rachel blows this opportunity, she's nuts," Nancy says. "She should have been on the next plane back to California after David proposed. If she waits too long, he's going to change his mind again."

"I don't think she's worried about that," Cheryl says.

We don't see Rachel again till after dinner. She comes back to our room about nine. Nancy's left finally, and her magazines are scattered all over the floor. She seems to think we're her maids.

Rachel comes in and sits on my bed. Her eyes are red and swollen, and she looks tired. "I've finally decided," she says. "I can't marry David. It's too late now. Too much has happened that I can't forgive him for. It wouldn't be good for me or the baby."

"Are you sure?" Cheryl asks her.

"I'm sure," she says. She takes a deep breath and exhales loudly. "He's a no-good bastard. I hate him. I can't marry him. He can go to hell." She seems a little more cheerful after she says that. But she still looks worn out and something else I can't quite explain. Beaten, maybe. I wonder why. She could have married David if she wanted to. At least she had a choice.

"Did you play that album all afternoon?" I ask. "Did it help."

"It didn't help one goddamn bit. I couldn't find one frigging answer in that whole goddamn album," she says.

"I'm sick of every one of the songs in the album and I never want to hear them again."

Thursday at our group meeting Rachel tells us she has something to say.

"I've decided to give up my baby for adoption," she says. "I thought all of you should know."

She doesn't look up after she says that. She stares at her hands. No one says anything.

Unnatural, I think. That's what Rachel's always said. It's unnatural to give up your own child. Unnatural and inhuman. She could never do it. She wouldn't give up her baby for anything. I try to look at Rachel's face so I'll see something there. I need to see her so I'll understand.

"I finally had to admit to myself that I couldn't do it. I wouldn't be any kind of a mother—I'm not ready for it. I don't want to have the baby and then resent it."

"When did you change your mind, Rachel?" Mrs. Landing asks.

Rachel shrugs. She doesn't answer the question.

"I wanted things to be different," she says. "God, I wanted them to be different. I didn't want to give my baby to total strangers. I didn't want him to spend the rest of his life wondering who I was and why I gave him up. I wanted to keep him and love him. I wanted to do that, whether I was with David or not."

Her hair falls across her cheeks, hiding her face. "That's why I didn't have an abortion," she says. "Because I wanted to keep my baby. I thought I could make him happy, and he'd be someone for me to love. Then I started thinking that I was being selfish. That's what Mrs. Harris told me—and I began to think that she was right. I wasn't thinking about the baby. I was thinking about myself.

"So—I don't know what happened. I guess I finally figured out that I can't do what I want. I can't go back to California with my baby. He wouldn't have any kind of future there, and neither would I."

It's unnatural. That's the word that echoes in my head again and again. It's all unnatural. I still can't see Rachel's face, because it's buried in her hands. But her face has looked different the past few days, haunted and sad.

I sit there and think of how strong Rachel used to seem and how sure of herself. She always drove me crazy with her big mouth and all her opinions and bossiness and liberal ideas. She drove me nuts, but at least I knew who she was. After yesterday and today, I don't know who she is any longer. I can't connect the Rachel I thought I knew with the Rachel who screamed and cried and seemed to feel as terrible and confused as I did. I never thought about Rachel's loving her boyfriend the way I had, or feeling alone and bitter and sad and wanting to be loved. I never thought she'd give up her baby the way the rest of us were going to.

I'll tell you what's strange. When Rachel talked about California and Bob Dylan and women's rights, I thought she was a fool. But there was something nice about that. I didn't have to like her or feel bad for her. At least I could think that she was strong and tough, the way Nancy was, and she was going to leave this home without being torn apart and desperate the way the rest of us were. I wanted to think someone else was strong. Maybe I wanted Rachel to believe she could change the world—even if I thought she was crazy for trying. Maybe I wanted the world to change and get better, even though I knew it never would. I didn't want everyone else to be a pessimist the way I am. I wanted someone else to be strong because I knew I couldn't be.

I look at the top of Rachel's head and hear the sound of her crying. It's a lonely, isolated sound, because no one else is saying anything.

On Friday, I spend several hours playing poker with Cheryl and Rachel and Nancy. It's easier to learn the rules when you aren't drunk. I'm actually good at it. When we finally finish, I have more buttons than anyone else.

"Maybe this should go on my college application," I say. "I could write, 'While spending several months at an unwed mothers' home, I learned to play poker quite well.' That beats lots of other extracurricular activities I can think of—like band or the Latin club. At least they'd remember my application before they rejected it."

"Put it on your application," Nancy says. "That way you'll get lots of dates—when all the guys know you put out." Nancy's always saying things like that. She seems to think it's funny. She never seems to notice that she's the only one who laughs.

Other times she gets serious. She tells us how important it is for guys to think we're still virgins.

"You can never, ever tell anybody that you've had a baby," she says, as if we were going to go around telling the whole world about it. "Every man wants a virgin to marry. I don't know about you—but I'm gonna be that virgin."

Nancy's told us that about a hundred times too. She always grins when she says it. She thinks that pretending to be a virgin is funny.

"I've never met a man I couldn't outsmart," she says. "Thank God."

After we put up the cards, the four of us stay in the room together, talking occasionally. I look at the other three, and all of a sudden I wonder where they'll be a year from now. Nancy will graduate from Ole Miss by then. I'm sure she'll manage to snag a rich husband in the meantime.

I have no idea what Cheryl will be doing. She never talks about her future, and I don't want to ask.

Rachel, who's my age, is planning to go to college. Berkeley, she says. Her father is a professor there, she's told us over and over. She tells me I should apply there too. She's been bugging me about it ever since that old busybody Mrs. Harris told her what a high score I'd made on the National Merit test. "Your score's even higher than mine," Rachel said. I can tell it kills her. She's still shocked that anybody from Texas can tie her own shoelaces.

The funny thing is, I don't care. All of this used to be

important to me—being smart and getting high test scores and doing well. I thought it meant something. Rachel's told everybody how smart I am and now everybody seems to be treating me differently, and I don't even care. None of that matters anymore.

I don't know why I made that remark about my college application, since I haven't thought about college in weeks. Why should I? It seems a million miles away, just like the rest of my old life and my family and my stupid test scores and all the plans I used to make. I'm on a different planet now.

Eventually I'll go home. I know that. But I can't believe it sometimes. Everything in my life is divided up—before birth and after birth. I can't imagine what it will be like on the other side. I can't imagine what it will be like to go back.

"Do you ever wonder what our children will think of us someday?" Rachel says. She motions toward her own body and ours. Suddenly it seems like there are more of us in the room. There aren't four of us anymore, there are eight. I can almost see the other four, small and pink and helpless.

"Do you think they'll hate us for giving them up?" Rachel asks.

"I don't know," I say.

I don't want to think about my baby, but that's all I can think about these days. This is why I never think about college or the future or the rest of the world. They aren't important. All I can think about is my baby.

Some mornings I lie in bed and think about it. Is it a

girl or a boy? Who will he look like—Jake or me? Who will adopt him? Will they love him enough? Will they tell him he was adopted? What will they tell him about me? Will he ever think about me? And if he does, will he understand? Or will he hate me?

I try not to think about all of this. All it does is make me sad. The worst part is, I'll never know the answers to most of those questions.

Last year one of my teachers told me I had a "visual" mind, and I know it's true. I always make pictures in my mind. I can see myself and my baby now. We're moving upward toward together, in a straight line. Then I'll go to the hospital and have him, and we'll separate. Our bodies will part and so will our lives.

In my mind, it looks like a *Y*. He's on one side and I'm on the other. They call those lines rays in geometry. The two rays will go in different directions forever and they'll never meet. They'll just move away from each other, getting farther and farther apart. After a while, it will be hard to believe they were ever together.

My parents call over the weekend. They want to let me know they're coming here for Thanksgiving. We can all stay together in a motel in town, they said.

"I know it will help you to get away for a few days," my mother tells me. "And we want to come there to celebrate your birthday."

All the time my mother's talking, I look down at myself. My stomach is like a small mountain. I'm not sure I want my family to see me this way. I'm not sure they want to see me like this either.

"I can't believe you're going to be eighteen!" my mother says. "It makes me feel old to think I have a daughter who's going to be eighteen!"

I suppose it would make her feel even older to think about having a grandchild, too. But she doesn't mention that. Ever since I've been at the home, my family's never said anything about my being pregnant. I think the way they see it, the pregnancy is a problem they solved when I came to the home. For them, it's over and done with. I feel like they've almost forgotten about it.

They never ask me how I feel, and I never tell them. I never complain to them. I always have this strange feeling that they want me to tell them I'm feeling terrible. That way they'll know I'm being punished while I'm here. They want to make sure I've learned my lesson and I've paid for what I did.

This is just another goddamn piece of knowledge that I have and don't want. I want to believe that my parents love me, period. I don't want to think they'd like to punish me and make me as unhappy as I am right now.

Maybe they don't know how terrible I feel. But they aren't asking me, so there's no way they'll ever know. Or maybe they do know how awful it is for me and they think I'm getting what I deserve. There's no way I could explain it to myself and come to the conclusion that my parents love me. Maybe they both love the idea of me, and they don't especially like me as I am.

It's too confusing for me to think about much and too painful. All I know is that I don't want to see them and Pamela this soon before I have the baby. I can't think of anything worse than spending Thanksgiving together— the four of us. But no one's asked me what I think, and I don't see any way I can get out of it.

The Thirteenth Week
November 12-18

The weather's beautiful on Monday, so Cheryl, Rachel, Nancy, and I take our lunches outside. We sit on the porch and look up at the sky. It's a big, bright blue dome.

I can't eat much these days. Nothing looks good to me. Besides, everything inside me feels squeezed and pushed around. I don't think there's any room for my stomach.

So I sit and pick at my food and complain about it. Even if I was starving, I couldn't eat boiled okra. It lies on my plate like barfy penicillin mold. Mrs. Landing is very big on vegetables. Unfortunately no one's ever pointed out to her that they should be edible.

"God, I'm sick of being fat and pregnant," Nancy says. She's saying that every five minutes the past few days. It's getting boring for the rest of us.

She had false labor yesterday, whatever that is, and she

179

was pissed off when it stopped. "I'm ready to get this sucker over with," she says. She's smoking a lot since then, because somebody told her smoking brings on labor.

"I think Nancy's repressing her true maternal feelings about the baby," Cheryl told me later.

"What true maternal feelings?" I asked. As far as I can tell, Nancy has about as many true maternal feelings as a kumquat. Most of her feelings seem to revolve around herself.

I envy Nancy. I don't like to admit it, but it's true. It must be nice to bulldoze your way through life and just reach out and grab what you want and get rid of what you don't want and still sleep well at night. I wonder if you can become that sort of person by wanting it badly enough. Maybe I should work on it and become a new person. My new, optimistic personality is a flop anyway. I'm still very pessimistic. Maybe I should try something else.

"So who do you think is the worst-off girl at this home?" Nancy says.

She loves asking questions like that. She's always asking us things like who's gained the most weight or who wears the tackiest maternity clothes. It's pretty mean. But I usually join in so I can nominate Harriet for everything.

"I don't know," Rachel shrugs. "It used to be Gracie."

We hadn't seen Gracie again. She left for Boston, and her things were being shipped there. Mrs. Landing says

Gracie's living with an aunt for now and then she'll be going to a boarding school in January. She'll be in the seventh grade.

"Harriet," I say. "Definitely Harriet. When she finally figures out she's not a virgin anymore, she'll probably shoot herself. I wish someone would tell her so she could go ahead and do it."

"Shit," Cheryl says. Lately she's been swearing. I like to think it's my influence. "It's probably me."

"Screw you. It's me," Rachel says. She's always sworn a lot anyway.

"My parents hate me and I don't have anywhere to go," Cheryl insists. "After what I did, I don't have any friends left. Everyone in town knows about me. All of you are going to college, but I'm not. I have no idea what I'm going to do when I leave here."

We all stare at her. Her face is red and she looks as if she's going to cry, but she doesn't.

"I was only kidding," Nancy says. Cheryl shrugs and doesn't say anything.

"Well, hell," Rachel says. "My life's not that great either."

I can tell she's trying to make Cheryl feel better. The trouble is, Rachel's unbelievably clumsy about things like that. She's the kind of person who steps on your toe and tries to make up for it by shooting off one of your kneecaps. Then she tells you to look on the bright side and how you aren't really noticing your toe any longer, are you?

"I'll tell you why I'm the worst-off person in this entire home," Rachel says. "When I got pregnant, my shitty parents actually wanted me to have an abortion. They told me that would be better for everyone that way. They said I was lucky that abortions were easy to get these days."

"Yeah, well, big deal," Nancy says. "What did you expect? A medal?"

"Shut up," Rachel snaps. "You don't understand a goddamn thing about me. My parents got married because my mother was pregnant with me. So you know what they were telling me? They were saying they wished they could have gotten an abortion instead of having me. They could have avoided their whole crummy marriage and their awful lives together if they'd aborted me."

"That's not what they were saying," Cheryl says. She looks more concerned about Rachel than she is about herself. "They just wanted you to have more choices than they did."

"I knew what they were saying," Rachel insists. "They wished they'd had the chance to abort me. After I realized that, there was no way I could have had an abortion. It would have been like I was killing myself."

We all fall silent then. I take my fork and mash my okra into a slimy green paste. It looks even worse now. A few minutes later we pick up our lunch trays and go back inside. The day doesn't seem so beautiful after all.

On Wednesday, Mrs. Landing decides we need to talk about childbirth in our group meeting. The minute she launches into that topic, I wish I hadn't come. I don't want to think about giving birth until I absolutely have to. Next month, maybe.

Besides I feel like I've been through it already—with LaNelle and Donna and Gracie—and I know everything I need to know. I know it hurts like hell. I wonder if the doctors will knock me out cold if I tell them I'm extremely sensitive to pain. Maybe I can get a C-section like Gracie. That sounds easier.

Anyway, Mrs. Landing is really warming to the subject. She starts talking about very revolting things like "bloody show" and water breaking, and how you'll know you're going into labor when one of those things happens.

It scares me to death to hear her talk. I don't even like to go to the dentist, and this sounds a lot worse.

I think about having babies the same way I used to think about having sex. It seems like the world is divided up between women who've had babies and women who haven't. Once you have a baby, you're on the other side, and you have some kind of deep, secret knowledge you didn't have before. I looked at people like Donna and Gracie and wondered what they knew that I didn't. The trouble is, I don't want to have to go through childbirth to find out. I'd rather read a book about it. Reading is a much better way to find out about pain.

"Do we have to talk about this?" I ask Mrs. Landing. "I have a very sensitive stomach, and I may throw up if I hear much more."

Mrs. Landing smiles. "You're due next month, Anne,"

she says, "and so is Cheryl. Nancy will be having her baby any day now. I don't think we should put this off, do you?"

She seems very determined about the whole thing. That's one of her big points—education. We need to be educated about childbirth, blah, blah, blah.

I don't tell her my own personal theory that it's better not to know about bad things like pain in advance. Especially for someone like me, who's basically a big coward.

So I try not to listen. But I keep picking up words like *contractions* and *transition*. Transition sounds particularly bad. I wonder if I can skip it.

Mrs. Landing hauls out some awful diagrams of a baby being born, with its head moving downward. That's disgusting enough, but then she pulls out an honest-to-God photograph of a baby's head coming out from between it's mother's legs. Its head is bloody and gross, and all you can see of the mother is her two knees and some pubic hair. I start to feel faint.

"My God," Nancy says. "Was that woman nuts? Who took those pictures? Did they pay her anything?"

"It's educational," Mrs. Landing tells her. "I'm sure the woman agreed to do it to help other women giving birth."

"Well, I wouldn't take all the money in the world to be photographed like that," Nancy says.

"The discussion and pictures haven't helped me at all," I announce. "I feel worse now."

For once Mrs. Landing brushes aside our comments.

"I know how frightening this is to all of you," she says. "But it's something you're going to have to face, whether you like it or not."

She's acting very stubborn about the whole thing. She's getting mean these days. Maybe I'll stop going to these meetings if that's the way she's going to be.

We play poker again Friday night and I'm winning, when Nancy goes into labor. She times it perfectly, since she's losing badly and doesn't have any buttons left.

"The pains are about ten minutes apart," she says. "Let's keep on playing. Give me some more of those damn buttons."

"Take as many as you want," Rachel says. You can tell Nancy's making her nervous. Rachel shoves the button box across the table and most of the buttons spill out. "Take the whole damn box if you want," she says.

I've never played cards with anyone who's having a baby before, and it's nerve-racking. I start to lose immediately. I don't play very well under any kind of pressure. I glance at Nancy occasionally and hope this won't be as bad as those awful diagrams and pictures Mrs. Landing showed us.

Every few minutes Nancy lays down her cards and starts to breathe deeply, which makes it hard for the rest of us to concentrate. "I want to keep playing," she says. "It takes my mind off the contractions."

"What's it like?" Cheryl asks her.

Nancy pulls her hair back from her face and shakes

her head. "It's hard to describe," she says. "It's like a stom-achache that comes and goes."

After a while she puts down her cards and lies back on the bed. She's—what? the fifth girl I've seen in labor since I've been here? But I still don't know what to do or how to act. It's strange to be around someone who doesn't seem to be here. Every time Nancy has a contraction, her eyes look funny, and you can tell she's a million miles away.

Cheryl and Rachel and I stay with her the whole night. We can't do much. We just doze off and on, and bring Nancy glasses of water when she needs them. Sometimes I hear something and I wake up and realize she's been moaning. But she doesn't make much noise.

By seven the next morning, Nancy tells us she needs to go to the hospital. She picks up her overnight case and goes to tell Mrs. Landing herself. She acts like it isn't a big deal at all.

Rachel and Cheryl and I follow along so we can help. But there isn't anything for us to do. Nancy walks out to the car on her own with Mrs. Landing, and then she turns and waves to the rest of us. She looks perfectly calm.

We watch the station wagon get smaller and smaller in the distance. You can see forever out here. Rachel stretches and yawns. "I'm going back to bed," she says.

Cheryl and I wander back inside and have an early breakfast. We're the only people in the dining room.

I sit at the table and push my scrambled eggs around

on the plate. I cut them up into little pieces and try to eat them. They still taste bad. Everything tastes bad these days.

"You know what I'm thinking about?" Cheryl says. "I'm thinking about going to a secretarial school in Oklahoma City. I've heard they'll accept you there even if you haven't finished high school."

I can tell she's trying to make it sound good. It doesn't sound at all good to me, though. It sounds bleak and horrible. I feel guilty for having a home to go back to and for being sure that I'm going to go to college. I don't think it's fair. Cheryl should have the same chances I do.

"Secretarial school sounds interesting," I say. "It's very practical these days. Also, I think you'll probably be happier in a bigger city."

In a bigger city where no one knows anything about you. That's what I'm actually thinking. I know Cheryl is, too. Our conversation slows down after that, until Cheryl asks me what I think about Nancy.

"She seems to be able to get through all of this so easily," she says. "I mean, being pregnant and going into labor and having the baby. It doesn't seem to bother her that much. Do you think she'll still feel that way after she's had the baby?"

"I don't know," I answer. "I have no idea."

It's funny, but I hope Nancy will be fine. There's something nice about being around someone who hasn't gotten kicked and bruised and depressed the way Cheryl and Rachel and I have. For the hundredth time I wonder what it would be like to be stronger and tougher, like Nancy. But sometimes I think that we're all stuck with being who we are. It doesn't matter if we like it or not. We're stuck in some ways, and we can't change even if we want to.

The Fourteenth Week
November 19-25

Nancy had a baby boy. Everything went quickly and smoothly, Mrs. Landing tells us, and both of them are fine.

"Nancy said to tell all of you that labor wasn't that bad," she adds. "She's planning to be out of the hospital soon. She said the nurses don't like her because she's so attractive."

That sounds like Nancy all right. Having a baby hasn't changed her much.

We've been at our group meeting for about half an hour when the door flies open and Nancy comes strolling in the room. It's quite an entrance. She looks like a million dollars. Her hair's perfect as usual, and she's put on makeup, and you can't even tell she had a baby two days ago. She's wearing a hot-pink minidress

189

and white fishnet stockings that she must have been saving for months.

"I checked myself out of the hospital early," she announces. "I hate hospitals and that place is a dump, so I didn't see any reason to stay. Besides, I got tired of all those old-goat nurses trying to push me around."

She flashes a big white grin at all of us and comes in and sits down. She looks so good and confident that she's a big contrast to the rest of us. I feel even more pregnant and dowdier than I had before.

"Would you like to tell us about what happened, Nancy?" Mrs. Landing asks.

That's a pretty useless question. There's nothing Nancy likes better than being the center of attention. She settles back into her chair and grins again.

"Well, labor hurts," she says. "I should tell you that. But they've got lots of drugs they can give you so the pain isn't so bad. The good thing is, it goes quickly. I was only in labor for three hours after I got to the hospital. Even those witches they have for nurses told me that was pretty good for a first baby. They gave me an episiotomy, so I'm sore. You can get Mrs. Landing to tell you more about that, because I don't want to. What else? The food's terrible, the nurses are shrews, and I'm glad it's over with."

"So what was it like giving up your baby?" Cheryl asks.

For the first time Nancy's smile fades a little. "Well," she says, speaking slowly and carefully, "I hated doing it. But I knew it was something I had to get through. I just tried to do it as quickly as I could so I could forget about it. I didn't want to see him, because I knew that would make it harder. So I just made myself go ahead and sign the papers. I knew I'd feel better the minute it was done."

She sighs a little. "It's all over now," she says. "It's behind me."

After the meeting is over Cheryl and I talk to Nancy while she packs. Well, listen is more like it. She talks about going back to school in January and finding a new boyfriend since she's sick of all her old ones anyway.

Nancy tosses her head and smiles at us. "It's such a relief not to be pregnant anymore," she says. "I feel like I'm pretty again for the first time in months."

She stuffs the last of her clothes in her suitcase and slams it shut and locks it. She walks over and hugs and kisses Cheryl and me. She leaves a streak of pastel lipstick on Cheryl's cheek.

"I'll miss you both," she says. "I'll even miss Rachel. We had some good times here, didn't we?"

I don't believe what she says about missing us, exactly. I can tell Nancy's already putting us behind her too. She's finished with this place and everyone in it. She's moving on.

"I don't have room for all those stupid stuffed animals," she says. "Why don't you give them to the next poor soul who moves in here?"

My family comes to pick me up Wednesday, the day before Thanksgiving. I'm spying on them from the window in our room, and I can see them park the car and get out.

My parents act jumpy. Pamela's gawking around. I bet she wants to see some of the other pregnant freaks here.

I sit in my room for a few minutes and watch them and wonder if there's anywhere I can hide. Maybe I can hitchhike to the border.

But I don't, naturally. I walk out into the hall, and there they are. We hug each other and kiss. I can tell that makes all three of them more uncomfortable. They don't want to get close to me when I'm so big and pregnant. I can see Pamela staring at me when she thinks I don't notice. Pamela doesn't have a subtle bone in her body, except for her brain.

"Are you ready?" my father says. I can tell he wants to leave as soon as possible. This place gives him the creeps. He picks up my suitcase and heads out the door.

We drive into town, and all the way my mother and Pamela talk brightly. They yak about everything like the weather and school and people we know and movies they've seen. They laugh a lot, too. They talk about everything, except the fact that I'm eight months pregnant and big as a cow.

My father doesn't say anything, and neither do I. Our silence hangs there in the air, and my mother and Pamela rush in to fill it. They're practically acting hysterical.

"Bob and I broke up," Pamela says. "Can you believe it—after all the months we've been together? But I'm fine. I'm not sitting at home crying or anything. I'm dating Donny Henderson now. He's the quarterback this year, you know. He's a lot cuter than Bob, too."

The more she talks, the more I realize I haven't missed her at all. As a matter of fact, I can't believe we're sisters. Maybe we aren't, really. Maybe they got one of us mixed up at the hospital when we were babies. Me, probably.

My real parents are glamorous artists. They're sensitive, like me. My real parents would understand me. Right now they wouldn't be driving me to some dumb motel. They'd be telling me how much they love me and asking how I feel about having the baby. We'd all be laughing and crying together about how hard this is and how much it hurts us. If I were with my real parents, I wouldn't feel so alone.

My real father would be furious at Jake for hurting me. He'd threaten to take a shotgun and kill him. I know that doesn't sound like a sensitive artist, but artists are very temperamental and inconsistent. Maybe he would threaten to stab Jake with his paintbrush instead. That would be more artistic.

My real mother would cry and hug me and she'd tell me that I'm strong and brave. She and I would talk about being pregnant and having a baby, and how painful it is to give up your own child. She'd write a special poem for me and my baby and publish it in a literary magazine. We'd frame the poem and put it in my room at home.

But I don't have my real parents with me. I'm with these two impostors and some cheerleader they brought with them. All I can see is the back of my fake father's head. He doesn't say anything to me. He stares straight ahead and drives. My fake mother turns around to talk, but she isn't talking to me. She's talking to someone she wants me to be. I'm not sure what that daughter would be like. All I know is that she wouldn't be pregnant.

We pull into the parking lot of the only motel in town. It's made out of some kind of fake adobe, and it looks as old and decrepit as the Alamo.

My parents already checked in, and we have two rooms with a door between them. I tell everyone that I'm tired and need to sleep. I go into the room I'm supposed to share with Pamela and get into bed and pull the covers over my head.

The next day we have Thanksgiving dinner at a restaurant. The restaurant is called Sal's, and it usually serves Mexican food. Their idea of Thanksgiving dinner is about the worst meal I've ever had in my life. Whoever Sal is, he deserves to be deported. Anyone who serves this bad a Thanksgiving meal is probably breaking lots of immigration laws.

The turkey is gray and greasy, and it tastes like it's embalmed. The dressing is bright yellow, and there are canned cranberries and peas the color of army helmets along the side of the plate. My mother and Pamela say it's delicious. Pamela even has second helpings. At the rate she's going, she'll get fat sooner than I expected.

"It's so nice not to have to cook this year!" Mother says. "Maybe we should make this a new family tradition."

I play with my food and get more and more depressed

looking at it and listening to my family. Sometimes I think they're crazier than I am. What does Mother mean, a new family tradition? Does she want me to get pregnant again next year so we can all meet here again and get food poisoning?

My father pushes his plate aside and starts talking about politics. It's almost the first thing he's said since they picked me up.

"The Negroes are a big problem these days," he says. He acts like he's lecturing us. "A big problem. The more they get, the more they want. They've got all the welfare they want, thanks to that no-good president. And what do they do? They riot. I know a lot of people who think it's a good idea for them to go back to Africa. Maybe they should, since they think this country's so bad."

Fortunately I'm not eating anything when he says that. I would have sprayed it all over the table. I wonder what Rachel would say if she were here. She'd say my father is a typical southern bigot. She'd have a point.

"But Daddy," Pamela says, "lots of Negroes are good athletes. Our team wouldn't be nearly as good if there weren't Negroes on it. You don't want to see all the good players go back to Africa, do you?"

"Please," my mother cuts in. "This is a religious holiday. We shouldn't spend all our time talking about Negroes and politics. We should be talking about how grateful we are for all the blessings we have."

She smiles at all of us. "I'm so grateful for this wonderful meal," she says. "And I'm grateful to have our family gathered around the table. We're so lucky to be together! I wish my parents could be here too. That would have made everything perfect."

I almost die when she says that. That's typical of how Mother is completely nuts, talking about her parents and everything.

I try to imagine what it would be like with my grandparents here. It's already two o'clock, so Nana would be drunk by now. She usually holds off drinking till later in the afternoon. But holidays are special, and she likes to get an early start.

I wonder if Mother remembers the Thanksgiving two years ago, when Nana got loaded and out of control. Mother tried to hide her bottle of bourbon, and Nana caught her and got pissed off. So she bit Mother on the hand and it bled all over the kitchen floor.

Mother had to go to the doctor the next day to get it taken care of. She told the doctor that our dog had bitten her, and then she had to talk him out of giving her rabies shots. She said the dog was perfectly healthy, but he was a little high strung. Fox terriers were like that. The doctor told her she should think about having the dog put to sleep, and Mother said she'd think about it if things didn't get better.

My father thought that was hilarious. He told Mother that maybe we could sneak Nana into the vet's office and pass her off as a fox terrier. "She looks exactly like one," he said. "We could put a collar on her, and maybe the vet wouldn't figure it out till it was too late and Nana'd gone on to pet heaven." Mother said she didn't find that humorous in the slightest, and she was sick of Daddy's making fun of her family.

Granddad doesn't bite or drink, but he's even worse than Nana in some ways. He comes to our house for holidays and complains about every meal he eats. "It's too bad all the women in this family are such damn bad cooks," is what he says. He sits around and refuses to eat, and then he tells my mother that she might possibly be the worst cook in the family.

Three years ago he got sick after Thanksgiving, and he was sure he'd gotten food poisoning from my mother's cooking. He suggested she'd done it on purpose so she could get his money. "I think I'm changing my will," he said. "I'm leaving all my money to the VFW. I'll tell you why, too. The meals I had in the army were the best I ever had in my life."

My father never said much when my grandparents were around. He went into one of his silent moods. But sometimes when it got bad, I could tell that maybe he was glad his parents were already dead and he didn't have to put up with any of this.

After my grandparents left, Mother would go into one of her horrible moods, and she'd stay in bed for a week. Then one day she'd get up and she'd have a bright, hard smile on her face and she'd start talking about how good it had been to have us all together for a holiday.

I used to wonder about that. Sometimes it seemed that whenever my mother looked at things realistically, she got depressed. It would take her a while to change things around in her mind. But finally she'd manage, and she'd convince herself that her parents loved her and that we'd had a great time together.

That was always weird for me. I never could figure out if it was better when my mother was depressed and realistic or when she was trying to be happy and was completely out of touch with reality. All I knew was I couldn't bear to hear her talk about how wonderful her parents were, and how much they loved her.

She has that same bright, hard smile on her face now. She looks through that face at the world, and she can't see a husband who doesn't love her and one daughter with the brains of an eggplant and another daughter who's eight months pregnant, and she doesn't taste the greasy turkey or the peas that are as hard as marbles.

Sometimes I think that's why I'm so pessimistic. Maybe I go through life seeing everything my mother refuses to see. I look at her now, and I see someone who's clinging to lies until her grip gives out and she breaks again. I look at my father and see he wants desperately to be somewhere else, anywhere else but here. I don't bother to look at Pamela. It's not worth it.

After Thanksgiving dinner we go back to the motel. It looks worse in the daylight than it did last night. I can't imagine what we're going to do here for the next three days. Maybe I can go into a coma.

The minute we get inside the door, my father sits down in front of the TV set and turns it on full blast to a college football game. I didn't remember him liking football that much. My mother asks him to turn down the sound so we can talk, but he ignores her.

So Mother and I go into the next room and shut the door. We can still hear the TV when the announcers shout and the crowd screams. It's a dull roar that comes and goes.

Mother and I sit down on the two beds, facing each other. "You look so pretty, Anne," she says. "I like the dress you have on. It brings out the color in your eyes. And I like the way you're wearing your hair."

That's supposed to make me feel good, but it doesn't. I wonder how long I can be around my family without anyone mentioning my pregnancy. I have the feeling I could probably go into labor right now and everyone would pretend not to notice. My father would turn the TV up louder and my mother would smile harder.

They don't want to look at me, and they don't want to hear what I have to say. For a few minutes at lunch I tried to talk about some of the girls at the home.

"It's funny," I said, "but some of them have become my friends. I feel so close to them."

My father looked at me strangely. Then he spoke to me for almost the first time since we'd been together. "I don't think they're the kind of people we care to hear about," he said.

After that I didn't say anything more. I can't imagine why my parents are here. They don't want to hear about my life or what's hurting me or about any of my friends at the home. We're all the kind of people they don't care to hear about. Why did they bother to show up, anyway?

Early Friday my father gets a call about one of his cases. "I have to go back to Dallas immediately," he tells us after he gets off the phone. "It's urgent."

He acts like he's a brain surgeon and somebody will die if he doesn't get back in the next ten minutes. That's a big joke. I'm sure it's just another one of his greedy clients who wants to cheat someone else out of ten bucks.

But Daddy starts throwing his stuff in a suitcase, and so do Mother and Pamela. They act like it's a big emergency too.

"We hate to miss your birthday," my mother says. "We wanted so much to spend it with you, Anne."

They drop me off at the home an hour later. They all kiss me again and tell me how wonderful it's been to see me. My mother presses a present and card into my hands.

I turn around before their car is out of sight. I can tell from the sound that my father is flooring the gas pedal so he can get away as fast as possible.

To hell with them, I think. To hell with all three of them. They aren't any more relieved to say good-bye than I am.

I walk through the front door of the home. For the first time in two days I'm back where I belong.

We've just finished dinner Saturday night when Mrs. Landing comes into the dining room. She's carrying a cake with candles on it, and I realize it's for me. Everyone gathers around the table to sing "Happy Birthday," and I manage to blow out all the candles without slobbering over the cake too much.

The cake is white with blue decorations. It says *Happy 18th, Anne!* in shaky blue writing. I know Mrs. Landing made it for me. That's nice, even though the cake is pretty awful. Mrs. Landing is an even worse cook than my mother. I've heard they try to keep her out of the kitchen as much as possible because she started a fire in the stove one time and the walls are still black. The icing tastes a lot like shaving cream, but we all eat it anyway.

I have two presents, from Cheryl and Rachel. Rachel gave me a paperback called *The Second Sex*. It's written by a French writer whose name sounds kind of familiar. Inside it Rachel wrote: *Dear Anne, This book has been very meaningful for me. I hope you read it, because you need to. Peace, Rachel.* Cheryl gave me a small bottle of White Shoulders cologne. That's nice, since I know she doesn't have any money.

Later that night Cheryl and I lie on our beds and talk. I tell her about seeing my family and how I'm probably an orphan, since I don't think they're my real parents.

"Things like that happen all the time in hospitals— getting babies mixed up, I mean," I tell her. "I've read about it a lot."

Cheryl doesn't seem convinced. "I saw your mother from the window, and you look a lot like her," she says. "Anyway, I still think you're lucky. At least your parents speak to you."

"Ha," I say. "Sometimes I think I'd be happier if I never saw them again. They'd probably be happier too."

I lie there and stare at the ceiling. I haven't checked the cracks in weeks. They're still big.

I can't believe today is my eighteenth birthday. I've tried to forget about it the whole day. Last year I never imagined I'd be spending my next birthday in an unwed mothers' home. But here I am. The funny thing is, I feel more comfortable here than with my own family.

Sometimes I wonder if I can ever go back to living with my family again. Maybe I should become a hermit instead of joining a convent. Or maybe I should hitch-hike all over the country and take lots of risks, like Rachel is always saying her friends do. "You get into the people that way," she says.

"You know, my parents never mention Jake's name," I tell Cheryl. "They act like I got pregnant by drinking bad water or something."

"You never mention Jake's name either," Cheryl says. "Except for that time you got drunk and started talking a lot."

I know she's right. I never want to talk about Jake because it hurts too much. Mrs. Landing still nags me about it. She says I'll feel better and I can start healing myself if I talk about it.

I didn't tell her I hate it when people use words like that—healing, I mean. It makes me think of a Band-Aid, and I don't need a Band-Aid. I need a shot of novocaine in my heart. In my next life I'm going to be heartless. That sounds wonderful. I wish my next life would start tomorrow.

"I'll tell you what's so damned ironic about every-thing with Jake," I say, and start to choke up. Boy, I hate that. I'm a complete mess. I was a seventeen-year-old mess and now I'm an eighteen-year-old mess. I don't call that progress. I also don't look forward to becoming a nineteen-year-old mess. The older I get, the more pathetic it sounds. Someday I'll be a middle-aged mess, like my mother.

I take a big breath and let it out loudly. "I'll tell you what's so damned ironic," I repeat. "I thought I was get-ting over Jake. I thought I was getting over him and that I was going back to my old life and I could close every-thing off. I was ready for it. Then I finally figured out I was pregnant. It made me realize that none of it was over. I was having a baby, and that meant that none of this would ever be over. I'd never get over him. It would stay with me forever."

Once I realized I was pregnant, I found myself looking closely at babies and children and adults. I wondered how they'd come to be. I always had the dim idea that it took love and some kind of caring to make a baby, and that most babies were born because someone wanted them.

When I got pregnant, I realized it didn't take anything like that. Babies could be some kind of sad, ugly acci-dent. That made me look at other people differently. I wondered which ones were the accidents. I wondered if they knew they were accidents and that no one had wanted them, ever. My mother always told me that

Pamela and I had been planned—but who knew? My mother lied a lot, and maybe this was just another one of her lies.

As long as I'm talking about lies, I have to admit it isn't exactly true that my parents never mentioned Jake. After she found out I was pregnant, Mother always called Jake "him," like she couldn't bring herself to say his name. "I can't believe you let him do this," she said once. "How could you do this to us? After all we've taught you and everything we've done for you—you let him do anything he wanted and you threw it all away. Do you know what you've done to us? Do you even care?"

By the time she finished saying that, she was screaming. She called me "a little idiot" that time. She said I didn't respect myself or them or anyone else.

A few times she threatened to call Jake and his parents. I told her I'd kill myself if she did that. I didn't want Jake to know I was pregnant. That was going to be my secret from him, always. I don't know why. I just knew that I never wanted him to know how much I loved him and how much he hurt me and that I was carrying something he and I had managed to make together.

By that time I was bluffing, though. I didn't want to kill myself any longer. I didn't want to die. The problem was, I had no idea how I was going to live.

The Fifteenth Week
November 26–December 2

Two new girls arrive this week. One is from Louisiana and her name is Velvet, of all things. The other's from Fort Worth, and her name must be even worse than Velvet, because I can never remember it. They're both about my age, but they seem a lot younger.

Both of them come to our group meeting. The funny thing is, I don't dislike them. I just realize that I don't want to get to know them. I don't want to get to know anybody new. I feel like I'm pulled in too many directions already, and I can't be stretched any further. I know I care too much for my baby, and I'm going to have to give him up. I feel close to Cheryl and Mrs. Landing and sometimes Rachel, and I know I won't be seeing them again after I leave. I even miss Nancy.

I've never had friends like I have here. I've never felt this close to other people before. It's nice to know I have friends, but it's terrible to think we'll never see each other again. I have no idea how Mrs. Landing gets to know people and says good-bye and then meets new ones and somehow manages to care about them. There's no way I could do that. It would hurt too much.

I like a few people here, and that's enough. I don't want to make any more friends that I'll never see again.

Last week Mrs. Landing told me she thought I was more "mature" than most of the other girls. That made me suspicious. I could tell she was working up to something and I was right.

"Since you've matured so much and you've worked through so many of your problems, you could really help some of the other girls," she said. "Especially some of the newer ones."

I almost choked when she said that. As far as I can tell, I haven't worked through one goddamn problem since I've been here. Sometimes I think my problems have gotten worse. I don't think Mrs. Landing thinks I've matured that much either. I think she has some half-baked idea that I'll get better by helping other people. She's very big on plans like that. I don't have the heart to tell her she's nuts. Sometimes I wonder if that's what she's done with her life—tried to get better by helping other people.

But I keep going to the group meetings because they make me feel better. I don't feel as lonely when I'm there. When I go to the meeting today, Velvet and the other new girl are talking about themselves.

Velvet has bright orange hair that God didn't give anyone, unless he was in a very bad mood. Her face looks
like she puts on her makeup with a broom, and she's
plucked her eyebrows into tiny lines that make her look
surprised all the time.

Velvet claims that her boyfriend, Chuck, wanted to
marry her. But she told him she didn't want to start out
married life with a baby. I try not to roll my eyes when
she says that. Velvet strikes me as the type whose name
and phone number are in every men's room in town. I
wonder if she could pick the father of her child out of a
police lineup. Come to think of it, that's probably where
she met him.

Then the other girl speaks. Her name is Johnny Ann.
She has lank brown hair and a bad complexion. She says
her parents tried to force Billie Don, her boyfriend, to
marry her.

"It was awful," she says. Her voice is high pitched and
nasal, like a teakettle. "My dad's a deputy sheriff, and he's
a pretty good shot when he isn't hung over. The next
thing I knew, Billie Don had up and joined the army and
left town."

I almost get a migraine when she tells that story. Talk
about tawdry. When you put two people together who
have double names, you must automatically come up
with a trashy story.

"I did get a postcard from Billie Don, though," Johnny
Ann says. "He said he decided he'd rather go to Vietnam
than mess with my dad. It was a nice postcard, with a

pretty picture of a bridge on it. It came from San Francisco, and he signed it, 'All my love, Billie Don.' He said he hoped I was doing well too."

Listening to the two of them, I realize they need more help than I can give them. I'm glad I decided not to get to know them better. "Good Lord," I say later to Rachel and Cheryl, "this place is going downhill fast. Johnny Ann's so dumb they should have dropped her off at the ASPCA. Actually Velvet too. With her moral standards she'd fit in just fine."

That makes Rachel mad. She's been in a terrible mood ever since she read that Julie Nixon and David Eisenhower are engaged. "They're going to have a million kids, and they'll all be Republicans and they'll all want to be president," she said several times. "This country's doomed."

Right now she's mad at me, though. She starts complaining about how everyone always talks about women's moral standards and never about men's.

"And now you're doing the same thing, Anne," she says. "Haven't you even bothered to read the book I gave you for your birthday? You could have learned something from it."

I'm in a bad enough mood that I tell Rachel I'm sick of her stupid sermons about society and everything else she bores people to death with. "You talk and talk and talk, and nothing ever changes. And you can take your damn book back if you want to. Why don't you give it to Johnny Ann? She can spend the rest of her life sounding out the words."

For about five minutes I feel better after I said that. Maybe I'm developing the new personality I've been thinking about and I'm not passive-aggressive any longer.

But then I begin to feel crummy. Ever since Rachel decided to give up her baby, I've felt differently about her. I think I finally understand her now. She tries to act a lot tougher than she is, the way I do. But we're both like marshmallows inside, squishy and soft. I hate being a marshmallow, and I think Rachel does too.

I know I hurt her feelings, so I go to her room to apologize. I say I know I'm crabby these days. "But I didn't mean to hurt your feelings," I add. "And I think the book looks interesting."

That's a complete lie. I read about two sentences of that book and decided it was the most boring thing I've ever seen in my life. I like books with plots and characters I want to be. This thing was like reading the *Encyclopaedia Britannica*.

Rachel doesn't answer. She just looks down, like she's drooping. Everything in her room seems to be drooping too. All the posters she put up on the wall are almost falling down. It's a sad sight. Since she isn't talking, she must be mad at me. I hate it when people are mad at me.

"I'll tell you what gets me," Rachel says. "You're right about some things, you know. I don't think anything's changed at all."

"What do you mean?" I ask.

She shrugs and then her shoulders sag. "I feel like

everyone's let me down," she says. "David and my parents and the whole damn world. Especially my parents. I always thought they were different from other people— better, I mean. They made a big point of letting me know how liberal they were about things like sex. And then they acted like it was the end of the world when I told them I was pregnant and I wanted to keep the baby. My father said that maybe he should get one of his friends to give me a psychological evaluation, since I seemed crazy. It made me realize that my parents were creeps and hypocrites, just like everyone else's parents. Like yours. Sometimes I wish I'd gotten an abortion. I don't want to bring a baby into this dirty, stinking world."

Rachel starts crying. Everybody is crying these days. I'm as bad as everybody else. Lately I've been spending about half my waking hours crying.

Then Rachel starts to bawl. She huddles up in some kind of big, pregnant bundle and cries for a long time.

I stay with her, but I don't say anything. That's the best thing to do, I think—just to stay with someone. I think about telling Rachel that her parents don't sound as bad as mine. But I don't think that would help much.

It's strange to me that Rachel still keeps talking about things like society and women's roles. She always tells us she's very idealistic, like it's some kind of wonderful thing to be. "The rest of you aren't idealistic at all," she says.

When she first said that, I thought it was true. I knew I wasn't idealistic. I didn't spend any time thinking about society or the war or all those big issues that Rachel was always harping about. I didn't go around thinking that it was important to change society. I was too busy worrying about myself. It's hard to be idealistic when you're thinking about yourself all the time. That's another one of my personality problems.

But now I'm not so sure Rachel is right about us. In a way all of us were idealistic, except for Nancy. We believed in things that seemed big to us. I believed that someone could love me and everything would turn out all right and I'd be happy. Cheryl believed in religion and that creepy minister at her church, and Donna believed in Dick, and LaNelle believed in something too, I'm sure. Maybe that she could make her baby's life better by giving her up. I don't know. I'm tired these days, and I'm not thinking well.

But I know we were all idealistic about something, and it ended up hurting us. Like I said, Rachel's a friend now, and I feel bad for her. But I don't think she's crying about society or any of those great big ideas she likes to talk about. She's the same as the rest of us. She was idealistic about one or two other people, and look where it got her.

The rest of the week I don't want to do anything. I want to lie in bed and feel grumpy by myself. Every time I lie or sit down, I feel like I'll never be able to get up. My stomach is like a beach ball that's about to burst, and even my feet are beginning to get puffy. I hate having puffy feet.

On the bright side, my breasts have gotten a lot bigger.

They actually bounce sometimes. I've never bounced in my life. Harriet says that never lasts, though.

"One of my cousins got really gigantic breasts when she was pregnant with her first baby, and then poof, they were gone after she stopped nursing," Harriet says. "She didn't have anything left, and what she did have sagged. She's looking forward to getting pregnant again so she can grow them back."

I'm sick of hearing about Harriet and her whole breeder family. As far as I can tell, all the women in her family do is lie around and read the Bible and get pregnant. It's pretty clear what the men spend their time doing, but Harriet never talks about them. Maybe she hasn't figured out what they have to do with it.

I'm in a bad mood, just thinking about Harriet and how my breasts are about to shrink any day now, and then Mrs. Landing comes in my room. She tells me I have to see Mrs. Harris today.

"Mrs. Harris is very worried about you," she says. "She's concerned about the way you always get sick when you have an appointment to see her. She said it would be understandable if it had happened once or twice—but six times is a little excessive. She's afraid you have a bad attitude."

I don't say anything. I just sulk. If Mrs. Harris had any idea how bad my attitude is, she'd wear a bulletproof vest.

"She said she was disappointed, because she thought the two of you were becoming good friends," Mrs. Landing says. She looks serious when she says that. But I have the feeling she thinks it's funny.

Well, I don't think it's funny. Not at all. And I feel even grumpier when I go to Mrs. Harris's office an hour later. She comes up and holds out her hands and grabs both of mine and squeezes them and gives me a big, gaping grin so I can see every filling in her mouth.

"Anne—how are you?" she says. "I've been thinking so much about you lately!"

I want to barf. I wonder if it's too late to say I'm getting sick again, right on schedule.

But I don't say anything. I put on that tight little smile I always get when I want to scream, and I wonder if I'm turning into my mother. Maybe when I have the baby and check out of the hospital and go home, everyone will think my mother and I are twins. That would make my mother happy. She's always wanted me to be more like her.

"Anne, I've been worried about you," Mrs. Harris says. That's about the twentieth time she's used my name in the first minute. Maybe she's going for some kind of social worker record. "I haven't seen you in weeks," she adds. "I want to make sure you know how important it is to talk about everything you're going through. I know you're making the right decision for your baby— but it's a hard decision to make, Anne. Not many people realize that."

Fortunately once she starts, Mrs. Harris is so in love with the sound of her own dippy voice that she keeps on yakking. That must be a social worker's idea of communication. I sit on my hands so she won't try to yank them again and give me that meaningful squeeze.

I look at Mrs. Harris and concentrate. I can tell she thinks I'm hanging on every word, but I'm actually trying to figure out what kind of barnyard animal she looks like. She's hard to classify, mainly because of those glasses that make her eyes look as big as billboards. I can't decide if she looks more like a goat or a horse. Maybe I should ask Mrs. Harris what her father's name is. If it's Fury, I'll know for sure.

I glance down at my watch and I'm surprised to see it isn't midnight. Mrs. Harris is all wound up now. Words and paragraphs come pouring out of her mouth, along with an occasional spray of saliva, and I wonder if she's trying to water the plant on her desk.

When I bother to listen, I realize she's talking about what a bright future I have. I almost get sick for the second time when I hear her say that.

"You're a smart, smart girl, Anne," she says. "A very smart girl." She seems to think something has more impact if you repeat it over and over, like the "Hallelujah Chorus."

"You'll leave here and you'll put your life back together and go on to a good college," she says. "We'll hear about you someday. I mean that very seriously, Anne. You're going to make your mark. I know it."

I feel sick and depressed when Mrs. Harris says that. I know what's in my future, and there isn't anything bright about it. I know what's going to happen to me. I'm going to go to the hospital one day soon and have my baby, and then I'll never see him again.

Right now I'm feeling stretched and pulled over every inch of my body. But at least there's something inside me. There won't be anything there after I give birth. I'll have my baby and he'll leave and so will I, and I'll go back to my family and I'll be alone again and every part of me will be empty.

I hate Mrs. Harris. She doesn't know anything about me or my future. I watch her lips move, but now I can't hear anything more.

I go to see Thomas on Saturday. I have to see him every week now, since I'm getting closer to my due date.

Due date. I'm sick of hearing those words. That's what everyone is talking about these days—Rachel and Cheryl and Harriet and Mrs. Landing and now Thomas. I don't want to think about my due date. I don't want to think about anything. I want to be left alone and roll up into some kind of pregnant ball and never let go. I'll go into fetal position with my baby and I'll never come out, no matter how much it hurts.

"You're dilated a little," Thomas says.

Dilated. I hate the word dilated too, even when Thomas says it. It makes me think of what they do to your eyes when they're trying to get you to wear glasses. One time my eyes stayed dilated for two weeks and I had to wear sunglasses everywhere. After that I hated to get my eyes dilated, and I don't want any other part of my body to be dilated, either.

"You know what that means," Thomas says. He looks at me intently with those beautiful eyes.

I'm sure Nancy is wrong about his being homosexual. I don't think he'd look at me that directly if he was homosexual. I've heard that most homosexuals just look down at the floor so they don't have to look at girls. Or maybe he's homosexual and it doesn't matter to me. I haven't been doing that great with heterosexual men, anyway. As far as I can tell, most men don't like girls that much, no matter what they say.

My mother never told me that "men want just one thing out of you," the way Cheryl's mother had. But she implied it. Maybe it's better when they don't want anything out of you.

Not that I care. I'm back to thinking about the convent idea. I wonder if they'll raise a fuss when they find out I don't believe in God. That might be more of a problem than never having sex again. At the rate I'm going, I don't want to have sex again for the rest of my life.

"You could go into labor at any time," Thomas says.

I can't help it. I feel tears rolling down my cheeks, and I begin to cry harder and harder. That's all I want to do for the rest of my life, for the rest of my bright future, is to cry.

When I can finally talk again, I tell Thomas I don't want to go into labor. I start crying again, and he pats me on the shoulder and tells me I'm going to be all right. He says he knows I don't believe it now, but I'm going to be all right.

The Sixteenth Week
December 3-9

It gets cold all of a sudden this week. At night you can hear the wind howl outside and feel it sweep in under the doors. The home isn't what you'd call insulated, and it stays pretty cold inside.

Rachel claims that one morning she got up and she could actually see her breath inside her room. Harriet says later that Rachel is hallucinating after all the drugs she's taken.

"I've now decided that Rachel is a drug addict," she tells Cheryl and me at breakfast one morning. "I read an article about it that said your eyes don't always stay dilated when you take drugs. People like Rachel who don't know the Lord are much likelier to become drug addicts. The article said that atheism is a very big risk factor."

217

I want to slap Harriet as usual. It's about time somebody does. I guess it's up to me, but I've never been too big on physical violence. So I tell her that I think taking drugs sounds a lot better than getting to know Jesus.

"I kind of prefer heroin myself," I say. "You should think about it, Harriet—it might improve your personality. Do you want to see my needle marks?"

Even Cheryl thinks that's funny. But Harriet's cheeks turn bright pink and she tells me I'm the most hateful person she ever met.

"I hope your baby goes to a good Christian family," she says. "It's going to need a lot of help to overcome its bad fortune in having you for a mother."

She gets up and leaves. She must think she's given me a mortal blow or something. But I don't feel that way. Harriet is one of the few people I know who can't hurt me much.

It's actually a relief to hear all the spite and nastiness in her voice. I've always known it's there, but she usually manages to cover it up. She's like some kind of sickly sweet caramel wrapped around a poison seed. The next time I see her, I'm going to say I've been praying for her every time I take heroin and God told me her baby is going to be the next Messiah.

"Do you ever think about that much?" Cheryl asks. "Do you think about the kind of people who'll adopt our babies?"

"Never," I say. That's a big lie. I'm turning into a constant liar. Every time I open my mouth, I seem to be

lying. I'm going to have to stop talking. "Well, some-times," I say.

Cheryl finishes her orange juice. That's all she's having for breakfast. Neither of us can eat much these days. I feel like my stomach is the size of a dime.

"I'm thinking about it a lot these days," she says. "It's so strange to me to carry a baby for so long and then give it up. You know, it comes out of your body and then it disappears, and I keep wondering where it's going to go."

She turns and looks at me directly. "Do you think they—the new parents, I mean—are going to love my baby? Do you think they can love a baby that's not their own?"

"Of course they can," I say quickly. This time I'm not lying. I believe what I'm saying. Sometimes I look at all of us—me and Cheryl and Rachel, anyway—and I think that we've done pretty badly with our "real" parents. I don't think people who adopt a baby will be any worse. And maybe they'll be better.

"At least you know that they want a baby," I say. "That's worth something."

"But don't you ever wonder what they'll be like?" Cheryl says. "Don't you wonder what they look like and where they live? What if we could choose them? What would we want?"

I know what I want. I want Cheryl to stop asking all these goddamn questions that I don't want to hear or think about. I can't stand this conversation anymore.

"This is stupid and useless," I say. I know I sound cross

and mean, but I can't help it. "It won't do you any good to think about who's going to adopt your baby. You're not going to have any choice anyway, so why think about it?"

Cheryl looks at me strangely. That makes me even angrier. "You're scared to think about it, aren't you?" she asks.

Oh, great. What's she doing, practicing to be a social worker? That's all I need in my life. Another prying, know-it-all social worker. This place is crawling with them. They can all go to hell and leave me out of it.

"I'm finished with breakfast," I say. I get up and leave by myself.

I almost go to sleep during our group meeting on Wednesday, except I'm too irritated to sleep. Johnny Ann is the only one who wants to talk, and she seems compelled to tell the world about every tiny thing that's ever happened to her. She's probably led the most boring life I've ever heard about. I can tell that getting pregnant has been the high point of her life, unless you count her father's drinking problem, which is very boring too.

"He gets drunk in front of the TV every night and just falls asleep," she says in her whiny voice. "Mama and I keep asking him to at least turn off the TV before he passes out, but he always forgets. That makes our electric bills real high."

Johnny Ann has very vacant-looking, pale blue eyes. I practice squinting at her so I can make her face disappear, and I notice she looks better that way. From where

I'm sitting, her face looks like a hard-boiled egg that's peeled badly. Someone should tell her eggs aren't supposed to have mouths.

Then Harriet starts waving her hand and jumps in to announce that she isn't dilated or effaced yet. She seems to think that's of great interest to everyone. She also repeats her story about all the women in her family having such competent cervixes, which is why her baby will probably be overdue.

I'm thinking about saying that Harriet's cervix is the only competent thing about her when Cheryl starts talking. She says she's been wondering about her baby's adoptive parents.

Wonderful. Just what I want to hear about again. Cheryl's doing this just to be mean to me. Maybe she's becoming passive-aggressive too. I wonder if it's catching.

"Sometimes I think about the parents I'd like for my child to have," Cheryl says. "I try to imagine them. It doesn't matter what they look like—but it would be nice if my baby looked like them. You know, like they all belonged together. But what I want most is for the parents to love each other. They've probably been trying for years to have a baby, and getting my baby will make them so happy. I like to think of how happy they'll be when they come to the hospital and see the baby and get to take him home with them."

Sometimes, Cheryl says, she thinks about what the parents must be doing now. "Maybe they're decorating the baby's nursery and buying diapers and clothes," she goes on. "Maybe a friend gave a shower for them after everyone heard they were going to be adopting a baby. I like to think about their having a shower sometimes. I like to think how happy everyone must have been."

The more she talks, the more bitter I feel. It sweeps over me so completely I don't know if I can stand it. How can Cheryl talk like this? How can she think about the people who are going to be taking our babies—and still be nice about them? When I think about those people for even a few seconds, I hate them. They're going to be happy and I'm going to be miserable. No, they're going to be happy *because* I'm miserable. There's a relationship here. Their happiness depends on my unhappiness.

What are we, anyway—all of us girls sitting around in this stupid, crooked circle? Cheryl and Harriet and Rachel and I are enormous now. Big with child, the Bible calls it. Big with someone else's child. We might as well be petri dishes or animals that have been bred. That's the way everyone sees us. We're being used until they don't need us anymore. No one cares about us afterwards—if we live or if we die or how we manage to get through the rest of our lives.

Harriet says all she cares about is that her baby is raised by a "good Christian family." Johnny Ann says she wants her child to have a father who doesn't drink and watch TV all the time. Velvet says something about the parents having enough money so her child can have "opportunities" she never had, whatever she means by that. A car, probably. Rachel doesn't say anything.

Suddenly I feel like I can't breathe. I hate all the people in this room. I hate everything. I feel furious and bitter and spiteful. I want to scream.

"It doesn't matter who adopts my baby," I say loudly. "I hate whoever it is."

Everyone turns and stares at me. They look like I shot off a gun in church or something.

Mrs. Landing nods at me. "Of course you do, Anne," she replies. "That's perfectly natural."

God, I hate it when people tell me what I'm feeling is "perfectly natural." There's so much goddamn stinking superiority to those words.

I can't believe I thought I liked Mrs. Landing. She's a creep, just like all the others. She doesn't understand me. Nobody understands me.

Cheryl doesn't either. I was right about her from the start. She's an ignorant little hayseed. Her philosophy of life makes Pollyanna look gloomy. She's probably planning to go out and get pregnant right away with some other minister so she can make another couple happy.

Nobody understands how terrible I feel and how much I hurt. My family is a bunch of mean, demented idiots. I still get letters from them every few days and when I open them, they talk about how they can hardly wait till I get back. A complete stranger could come in and read those letters and have no idea they're written to someone who's about to have a baby and give it up. They might as well be letters to a kid who's at summer camp. That's why I tear up most of them before I read them. They aren't for me anyway. My family doesn't care about me. Neither do my so-called friends.

I'm back in my room now, and I lie on my bed and start pounding my stupid pillow. I hope it breaks apart and makes a big mess. I have so much pressure in my chest, I feel like I'm going to explode any minute. I'm going to break apart too and make a big mess.

I look down and see one of my books. I pick it up and try to rip it apart, but it's too thick. So I throw it against the wall. It's a paperback, so it doesn't make much noise. But it feels good to throw it.

I gather up the rest of my books and start smashing them against the wall too. When they hit the wall, they make a splat sound that I like. I throw them harder and harder, faster and faster, and they make loud crunching noises. Then I throw my two pairs of shoes. They're rubber soled and heavy. They make a nice loud sound.

I empty out my drawers and throw my clothes against the wall. All those goddamn maternity clothes. I won't be wearing them much longer. I throw them so hard they make a whoosh in the air. That isn't enough noise when I throw my clothes, so I start shouting "Go to hell!" every time I heave something. I have a long list of people I want to say "Go to hell!" to, but fortunately I have lots of clothes. I work my way through my family and Jake and everyone at the home and the goddamn adoptive parents. I see their faces on the wall, and I hit them between the eyes every time. I hate them. I hate all of them. I want to hurt them the way they've hurt me.

I love throwing things. I haven't done it in years, and

it feels great. Once I empty out my drawers, I pick up my clothes and shoes and throw them again. I start down the list of people I'm saying "Go to hell!" to again. Whoosh, whoosh, whoosh, I smash them right in their stupid faces. I wish they were here so I could smash them in person. I wish I were throwing grenades. I lean down and pick up anything I can get my hands on and heave it against the wall. I grit my teeth and throw and scream until I can't move or make another sound. I stand there and look at the shipwreck of books and clothes and shoes all around me. What a mess, what a horrible mess it is, inside me and all around me.

All my energy and anger have finally drained out, and I collapse on the bed. I'm panting and exhausted, but I feel a little better. I said "Go to hell!" to lots of people who deserve it. I hope I haven't forgotten anybody. They can all go to hell and burn and rot there. I hate them.

The door opens and Cheryl comes in. She looks at my clothes and shoes and books scattered on the floor and at me lying on the bed with my arms and legs stretched out like a giant *X*. For a minute she looks shocked. Then she starts to laugh. After a few seconds so do I.

We laugh until our stomachs hurt and tears come to our eyes. Then both of us start to laugh and cry at the same time. We have tears rolling down our cheeks and we're laughing and sobbing and giggling and sniffling in the middle of a room that looks like a train ran through it and didn't even stop to pick up the pieces. We laugh and cry till there's nothing left inside, and both of us are quiet. Then we lie there and listen to the wind blow.

• • •

After that I feel better, but I don't feel great. I've started having those dreams again about the lost child. I always wake up crying after I have those dreams.

I can see the child's face even after the dream's over. I can't tell whether it's a boy or a girl, even though it doesn't seem to have any clothes on. What I remember best is its face—its big, scared eyes and its mouth that seems to cry with some kind of horrible helplessness. It has short, light-colored hair and it moves around a little and it's always looking for something or someone it can never find.

I try to get away from the dream and forget it. I climb out of bed and pull my robe on and wander down the hall, no matter what time it is. It's freezing cold in the hall, but I don't care. I pace back and forth in front of all the closed doors. There are dim lights along the hall-way, so I can see a little. I walk and walk and try to get away. Sometimes I even shake my head to try to empty it out, but other nights it feels too heavy to move.

There we are, my baby and I. We're walking together in the dark halls, late at night.

I wonder if babies have any memories of being inside their mothers. Maybe some kind of small, vague feeling or memory. Maybe so. Or maybe not. Probably not. We're walking together for one of the last times, and only one of us will remember it.

Tonight I feel as if I can walk forever, and maybe I will.

The Seventeenth Week
December 10-16

The weather is warmer and sunnier this week. For some reason that makes me feel better. I stop roaming the halls at night and begin to think they won't have to cart me off to the insane asylum once I have the baby. Some days I almost feel cheerful.

Mrs. Landing and Cheryl put up some Christmas decorations in the front hall. They've strung red and green streamers along the tops of the walls and a lopsided artificial wreath on the front door that rattles every time someone opens it. Mrs. Landing hauled out sheets of thick white cotton that look like snow and draped them across a table. Then she put a Nativity set on top of it.

The Nativity set looks like it's older than God. One of the shepherds doesn't have a head, which doesn't matter, since there aren't any sheep for him to herd anyway, and one of the camels doesn't have a wise man. I'm sure that symbolizes something. I'd ask Harriet about it, but she isn't speaking to me. She hasn't given me an update on her cervix in days.

"I guess Harriet's planning to give birth on Christmas Day," I tell Cheryl. "Have you noticed any big stars around lately?"

On Tuesday, Mrs. Landing has a Christmas tree dragged in. The two guys who bring it must have never been to an unwed mothers' home before. They scrape their feet and look down at the floor the entire time they're inside. They act like we're disfigured and too embarrassing to look at. A few weeks ago that would have bothered me, but now I don't care as much. I stand there in the hall with Cheryl and Rachel and watch them fasten the tree into the holder. At least the tree isn't artificial like the wreath. Every time I smell it I think of big green forests I've read about in books.

Wednesday night we have a tree-trimming party with decorated cookies and fruitcake that's at least a hundred years old and bright red punch. Cheryl starts worrying at the last minute that Rachel will be insulted because she's Jewish. But Rachel says all the important people in the Nativity scene are Jewish too, so she feels right at home.

We trim the tree with strung popcorn and a few rickety-looking ornaments and icicles and two strings of colored lights. Somebody puts a record of Andy Williams singing Christmas carols on the hi-fi, and Rachel says she objects to that on aesthetic grounds. We've drawn names earlier, and we place a few presents under the tree.

All of this is cheerful, which surprises me. Maybe

that's the good thing about never expecting to be happy. When you feel good—even a little good, like tonight—you're pleasantly surprised. I can't think what's making me feel peaceful and content about having a Christmas party in a home somewhere out in the country when I'm not religious and I'm about a million months pregnant and I haven't seen my feet in days. I guess it's because I feel like I belong here, and I haven't felt like that too many other times in my life. Maybe I'm more aware of it now because I know I won't belong here much longer.

Later that night, after everyone's gone to bed, I come and sit in the front hall. Everything is quiet and dark and peaceful. I turn on the Christmas tree lights and watch them twinkle in the dark. I think about this time last year, when I was so much younger and everything in my life was different.

My family spent Christmas at our house, and we had a big fire in the fireplace on Christmas morning while we opened presents. Daddy gave Mother a nightgown, which was what he gave her every year, and I wondered if he noticed she never wore any of them. But she said that was exactly what she wanted. Pamela got a necklace from Bob that she kept telling everyone was fourteen-karat gold, and we all gave Daddy ties and cigars as usual, since he didn't need anything.

The last present I opened was a tan cashmere coat. Inside the package was a card that said: *To Anne. A daughter who's done as well as you have deserves a special present. Love and Merry Christmas, Daddy.*

The coat was beautiful and expensive, and it's probably hanging in my closet right now. But it isn't the coat I remember as much as how it made everyone act. Mother got that tight, drawn look around her mouth, and I could tell that Daddy had bought the coat without mentioning it to her. She didn't say anything, but I knew she was wondering why he'd given me a coat like that and all he'd given her was some crummy nightgown she'd never wear. Pamela looked irritated too. The coat was much nicer than anything she'd gotten, and it took her at least ten minutes to recover and start babbling about her fourteen-karat-gold necklace again.

I hugged my father and thanked him. I knew what the coat meant. It was supposed to be a reward for me for doing so well in school, but it was also supposed to make up for a lot of things. Like not having a boyfriend, and having a mother who hated me and a sister who was practically retarded. I touched the coat and felt how soft it was, and it made me realize how much my father loved me.

That was almost a year ago, but it seems like forever and it seems like it happened to someone else. I barely knew who Jake was then. A few weeks later I met him and fell in love with him and everything in my life changed.

For months I've wished to God I never met Jake and ruined my life. I tortured myself over and over with how things could have been different. If I'd never met him. If I'd never loved him. If I'd never slept with him. If I'd been a different kind of person—better and stronger. If

I'd never gotten pregnant. If he'd loved me. Thinking about those things ripped into me and sometimes I could almost feel them inside me, eating at me and burning me.

One time after my mother had come back from the hospital, she and I had a good talk. Back then we used to have nice talks sometimes. For some reason I asked her what she regretted most in her life, and for a minute she looked wild and scared again, and I was afraid I'd done something awful and everything would start getting worse and she'd have to go back to the hospital. But then the look went away, and she shook her head and she said she regretted so many things she didn't have the time to talk about them. And she laughed in a strange way that sounded like a bark and said this was something she didn't want to talk about.

I saw then how many things were killing her, even if I didn't know what they were—and I never wanted to see that again. That was the way I've felt all these past few months too, since I'd been at the home. I had so many regrets I didn't want to think about or talk about, but they kept seeping in and poisoning me.

I know I could look back at that scene from last Christmas and wish that I was back there and I was the same person I was then and none of this ever happened. But for some reason I don't. I think about that scene and realize it wasn't as cozy or happy or wonderful as I wanted it to be. I'm not happy now, but I wasn't happy then, either. If I'm going to start regretting things, I know

I'd have to go back to the beginning and regret too many things about my life. It's not only Jake and getting pregnant I'd have to regret.

I sit here on the floor for what seems like hours, with my arms wrapped around my stomach and the baby, and watch the Christmas lights flash off and on. The past few months move slowly through my mind, bright and soft and painful.

I know it isn't any brilliant revelation to say that love hurts, but it does. I know that loving the baby is as crazy as loving Jake, but I can't help it any more than I could help loving him. In some small part of my mind I don't regret it, either. I haven't been smart about love, but I don't care anymore. I've been stupid and naive and blind and I've gotten hurt terribly and I know if I don't stop thinking about this, I'll start to sound like a country-and-western song. To hell with it. I don't care if I do. All the dumb mistakes I made have brought me here, gathered up like a ball and watching a Christmas tree blink. I realize, finally, that this isn't the worst place I've ever been.

Saturday morning I wake up feeling more energetic than I have in weeks. Cheryl and I decide to go Christmas shopping. Mrs. Landing is driving into town, and she says she'll drop us off in front of one of the stores and pick us up later.

Cheryl and I look pretty ridiculous, and I notice people staring at us sometimes, but I try to ignore them. We're both wearing coats we can't button, but it isn't that cold anyway. Cheryl's feet are so swollen that she has to wedge them into an old pair of loafers. Every few minutes she has to stop and sit down and rest her feet. I sit down with her and try to see my puffy feet, and we joke about how hard it's going to be to get back up.

These days I feel like I'm carrying around a watermelon. I try to imagine what it would like to be pregnant with twins, like Mrs. Kohler, one of our neighbors in Dallas. It kills me to think about it, and I decide to be much nicer to Mrs. Kohler in the future, even though her twin girls are very obnoxious and should be sent to reform school.

Between rest stops Cheryl and I walk from store to store, talking and trying on hats and looking at purses and anything else that you don't have to fit into. It's fun. It's one of those times it occurs to me I'm not a million years old, even though I feel like it a lot.

After an hour or so, I realize we're only pretending to shop. I don't especially want to buy anything for my parents or Pamela, and Cheryl's family still doesn't want anything to do with her. She's written them several letters, she told me, but her parents haven't answered any of them. "I guess I'll give up eventually," she said. "I guess that's what they want me to do."

I try to imagine the kind of parents who decide their daughter is dead. I wonder if you can look at them and see that kind of harshness in their faces. Or are they like LaNelle's father, and you can look at them and never see what they're really like? I'm sure that Cheryl's parents are the types who continue to show up at church every Sunday and listen to Pastor Browning talk about loving your neighbor and congratulate themselves for being such great Christians. I'm sure they still look up to that ignorant swine in the pulpit, too, who probably spends his afternoons getting hot and bothered by the Song of Solomon.

By noon I'm starving. I have to have food. I've heard about pregnant women who develop strange hungers and sometimes they even eat dirt. That's how I feel. I could eat dirt.

Instead we go to Ike's Coffee Shop, where we went when Gracie had her baby, and the food is at least a cut above dirt. I devour a greasy cheeseburger and I'm thinking about ordering a second helping of french fries when I notice Cheryl looks strange. I ask her what's wrong, and she says she's been having contractions for the past hour or so. "At least I think they're contractions," she says.

We decide we'll sit and wait. I'm still starving, but I don't order any more food. It doesn't seem polite to eat when someone is about to have a baby. So I try to talk a lot and take Cheryl's mind off what's going on, but I'm panicking. I'm not sure where Mrs. Landing is, and I don't know what we should do.

All of a sudden I wish I'd paid more attention to what she told us about childbirth. When are you supposed to go to the hospital? When your water breaks? (Yuck. I've always hated thinking about that.) When the contractions are—what? Ten minutes apart? Five? Is Cheryl having contractions anyway? Maybe not. Maybe it's false labor, whatever that is.

Great. Cheryl is about to have her baby, and I'm the one who should be in charge, and I'm practically in hysterics. I try to hide it by talking a lot. No, babbling is more like it. I talk about Christmas. I tell Cheryl I've never liked Christmas. I think it's because of my childhood. I had a very traumatic experience when I was eight. I was downtown shopping with my mother, and we walked past one of those Salvation Army Santas who ring bells and try to make you feel guilty. We walked on past him without giving any money, and naturally I felt guilty, because I always feel guilty anyway. Then I looked back at him and he was slipping some of the money into his pocket, and he saw that I noticed and winked at me.

"It was quite sleazy," I say. "It's a good thing I didn't believe in Santa then, or it would have messed me up. I told my mother about it and she said I must have imagined it. After that I've never given money to the Salvation Army. Who knows what those Santas use that money for? Child pornography, probably."

Cheryl smiles halfheartedly and tells me to keep talking. So I do.

I talk about books I've read and the vacation we took in the Rockies when the only fun I had was watching Pamela fall off a horse and break her big toe and how I once sent off for some of that boob cream they advertise in the back of magazines and it not only didn't work, I think I actually shrank after I used it. I talk about movies I like and movies I hate, and how my grandmother once tripped and fell down a whole flight of stairs and the doctor said she didn't hurt herself at all because she was so relaxed and drunk, and how I once spent ten dollars trying to win a stuffed animal at the state fair and all I got was a tiny horse and then I saw all the other girls wandering around with enormous stuffed animals their boyfriends had won for them. I talk and talk until my voice is about to give out and I'm boring myself to death, except I'm so nervous I can't feel bored.

Cheryl lets out a big sigh. It sounds like an explosion. "I've got to get to the hospital now," she says. "Everything's harder for me. It's hurting a lot more."

How are we going to get to the hospital? Cheryl can't walk more than two steps, and I have no idea where Mrs. Landing is. What are we going to do?

"I'll find someone to take us," I say, trying to sound definite.

I slide along the seat and squeeze out of the booth, which isn't easy. Three men are eating at the counter, and a crabby-looking waitress glares at me.

"My friend's in labor," I say. "Can anybody give us a ride? We need to get to the hospital."

The conversation stops abruptly and the three men swivel around. They look at me and then they look at Cheryl, who's laid her head on the table. If I've ever seen an emergency, it's the two of us.

"Good God," one of the men says. He stubs out his cigarette in the ashtray and slings a couple of dollars on the counter and stands up. "I'll take y'all, hon," he says. "I got a pickup truck outside, but I think we can all squeeze in the front."

He's what my parents call a country boy. He isn't any

taller than I am, even though he has boots on, and he has a grizzled face and gray hair with some kind of grease on it. But he looks beautiful to me. He pats his cowboy hat down over his hair and walks over to Cheryl. "You need help getting yourself up?" he asks.

Cheryl says no. She slowly eases herself out of the seat and stands up crookedly. The man takes her arm. "Lean on me, hon," he says. "It'll be a lot easier."

The waitress holds open the door. She still looks crabby. She must be dying to get rid of us before Cheryl has her baby in the booth.

The three of us slowly make our way to his truck. It's battered and light blue, with scraps of hay and God knows what else in the back. I hope I won't have to ride back there. Or worse, the way Cheryl looks, she might have her baby in the next thirty seconds and then she'll have to lie down back there and have it in public, and I'll have to cut the umbilical cord. That's all I need.

But the man manages to help her into the front seat, and then I get in too. It's tight and smelly inside, but it's better than rattling around in the back. We get to the hospital in just a few minutes, with the man honking his horn and running two or three red lights. I have the feeling he's enjoying it.

"Hang on, girls," he says as we skid around the corner. We bounce up and down and I wonder if they've ever heard of shock absorbers out here in the country.

We pull into the hospital emergency entrance, which looks familiar by this time. I'm practically an old hand at this, but it still scares me to death. The same two order-

lies, who seem to live here, come shuffling out. At least I
think they're the same orderlies. Maybe they all look
alike. I wonder if anything ever makes them hurry.
Lunch, maybe.

They open the door and look at me. "She's the one
who's in labor," I say, motioning toward Cheryl, who's
bunched up in the seat like a great big comma. That
seems to confuse the two of them. I don't want to wait
for a month until they figure it out, so I slide out of the
truck and push past them. "She's the one who's going
into the hospital."

They finally catch on and help Cheryl out of the truck
and through the glass doors. I follow closely behind. I'm
not sure I trust these two morons. They'll probably have
Cheryl scheduled for an emergency tonsillectomy if I
don't watch them. This is the first time I've been inside
the emergency waiting room, and it's surprisingly clean
and modern. But it has that awful hospital smell that
always makes me think of death and disease.

Cheryl disappears into another room, and I sink
down into one of the chairs. It's about as comfortable as
a rock. I leaf through some ancient copies of *Time* and
Newsweek and wish I'd gotten more to eat. I'm still hun-
gry and it doesn't look like I'll be eating anytime soon.

Someone taps me on the shoulder. It's the man who
brought us here. I realize I haven't even thanked him.
"You all right, hon?" he says. "Your friend all right?"

"I think so," I say. "I want to thank you for what you
did. It was so nice of you to bring us here."

He sits down beside me. He smells like tobacco and

coffee and fresh air all at the same time. He pulls out a pack of Marlboros and offers me one. I tell him I don't smoke, but I'm thinking of starting soon.

"Nah, don't start," he says, lighting the cigarette and inhaling. "It ain't something I'm proud of." He puts his cigarette down next to him and sticks out his hand. It's weathered and freckled, like his face. "Eddie Lee Brown," he says. "Pleased to meet ya."

"Anne Harper," I say, and smile. I like him. I feel like he saved our lives. I wish he'd adopt me. I don't want to go back to a city. I want to live here in the country, I decide just this minute. I want to run away and live here in the country with a new family.

He settles back in his chair and grins. "You know," he says, "this ain't the first time I rushed a pregnant woman to the hospital. Had to do the same thing with my wife. Our first baby came faster than we'd planned on. Course that was years ago, before you were born. But it brought them memories back, I'll tell you."

He takes another deep puff from his cigarette. "On the other hand," he adds, "I ain't never taken two pregnant women to the hospital before."

"We're both from the home," I say.

"I thought maybe you was," he says. "So I guess that makes this all different for both of y'all, don't it?"

I say yes, that makes it all different.

Mr. Brown stays here with me. I'm not sure why. Maybe he thinks I look lonely. That's it. I've now become clearly pathetic and people are starting to act nice because they pity me. I've gone straight from being passive-aggressive to being pregnant and pathetic. After I have the baby, I'll only be pathetic.

It's almost four when Mrs. Landing comes rushing into the room. "Good Lord," she says when she sees me. "You almost gave me a heart attack. I had no earthly idea where you and Cheryl were."

"Cheryl went into labor at lunch," I say. "This is Mr. Brown. He gave us a ride here. I think he saved our lives."

Mr. Brown stands up and shakes hands with Mrs. Landing. Then he touches me lightly on the shoulder. "I'm gonna go now."

I walk with him to the door. I thank him again and he tells me to stop. "I didn't do that much, hon," he says.

I shake his hand and I don't want to let it go. I don't want him to leave. He seems safe and reassuring, and I have to remind myself that I don't even know him. I look into his eyes and notice they're a soft, dark brown, like my father's.

"You just get through what you have to, hon," he says. "It ain't gonna be easy, but you just get through it and go on."

I stand at the glass doors and watch him get into his beat-up blue truck. He waves to me as he leaves.

I walk back and sit down by Mrs. Landing. I'm about to ask if we're going to stay here until we hear anything about Cheryl, but then I feel a strange, unmistakable gush.

Goddammit all, I think. So this is what it feels like when your water breaks.

• • •

I don't go into labor, but they check me into the hospital anyway. A bossy-looking nurse makes me sit in a wheelchair like I'm an invalid, and she takes me up to the second floor in an elevator. Then I get to lie in one of those awful hospital beds and wait. Every half hour nurses come in and bug me. They ask if I've had any contractions yet and when I say no, they act like it's my fault.

I don't want to talk to the nurses or anybody else. I want to leave and go back to the home. I hate hospitals. I'm not ready to have my baby. I'm not ready to go through all that pain, either. I'm scared to death, and I have to clench my jaw so it won't shake.

Thomas comes in at eight. It's so good to see him that I could cry. I want to jump out of bed and hold on to him. I don't think that has anything to do with sex or being in love with him. I just want someone to hold me for a little while.

I know I can't do that, so I tell him I want to check out of the hospital. "I'm not even in labor," I say. "They made a mistake admitting me. I can come back later."

He shakes his head and grins at me. "Didn't you read all those brochures I gave you, Anne?" he asks.

I say no, I haven't quite gotten around to them.

"Your water broke," he says. "That means you have to go into labor in a few hours—or it'll be dangerous for the baby. If you don't go into labor on your own, we'll have to induce it."

I don't like that word, *induce*. I'm not sure what it means, but it doesn't sound like anything I want to do. I also don't want to put my feet into those damn stirrups again, but Thomas says I need to.

He shakes his head while he examines me. "You're not any more dilated than you were a few days ago." The way he says it, I know that it's not good.

"If you haven't gone into labor by midnight, I'm scheduling you to be induced," he says. He's writing something on a clipboard. He pats me on my hand. "Don't worry," he says. "We can do lots of things for the pain these days."

Thomas leaves the room, and I try to watch TV. It doesn't help. I roll over and try to sleep, but I can't. Finally I get out of bed and walk down the hall. I wonder where Cheryl is. I wonder if she's had her baby. She didn't seem as scared as I am now. I've always been a very big coward. This is just another example of it. I've heard about women who scream their heads off during labor. I'm probably going to do that. I'll scream my head off and then die from pain and embarrassment. It will serve me right.

Maybe that will be better anyway, if I die during labor. There would be something romantic about that. The new parents could tell my baby that I loved him so much, I died from having him. They'll all love me for making such a great big sacrifice. My family will feel sad for about five minutes. Then they'll get over it. Maybe they'll feel guilty about the rotten way they treated me. I hope so. I wonder what Jake will think when he hears I'm dead. Maybe he'll be so upset that he'll go out and crash his car. Or maybe he'll just try to remember who I am when he reads my obituary. He'll look at my picture and think, Oh, yes, she looks familiar. I wonder if she was in my chemistry class. He'll never know that I died having his baby.

I feel sorrier and sorrier for myself. I've always been pretty bad about self-pity. Tears start oozing down my face. I don't want anybody to see me walking around and moping, so I go back to my room and lie down and cry myself to sleep.

The Eighteenth Week
December 17–December 23

A nurse wakes me up at midnight. At least I think it's a nurse. She'd make a great drill sergeant. Her name tag says she's Rose Ryan, LVN, and her face looks like one of those Mr. Potato Heads.

"Time to induce," she says. "Doctor's orders."

I'm about to tell her that I have a great fear of needles, but she's already winding some kind of rubber thing around my arm. I wonder if she knows that will cut off my circulation. I hope this hospital knows something about circulation. If she starts hauling out leeches, I'll know I'm in trouble.

"This'll only hurt for a minute," she says.

I shut my eyes. I can't stand to look at needles, especially if they're headed in my direction. She stabs me with something, and then she pulls off the rubber thing. I can hear her humming some song, like it isn't any big deal to go around stabbing people and practically killing them.

"Aren't you going to take the needle out?" I ask.

She seems to think that's funny. "The needle stays in," she says. "It's giving you stuff that's going to put you in labor."

Stuff? Great. I have an incompetent nurse who's giving me "stuff." She's probably completely illiterate, and she's giving me some kind of poison that will kill me. I lie there and wait to die.

Five minutes later the pains start. The first one rolls across me like someone's kicked me hard. What's strange is how it keeps on. It doesn't come and go quickly. It grabs me and holds on. Finally it stops and I lie there, panting. It feels good, for a few minutes, not to hurt.

Then I can feel something start to happen again. My stomach begins to ache and it feels tight and hard all of a sudden. The pain starts small and gets bigger and bigger. I clench my teeth and my hands and try to lie still. It rips through me like a saw and then it slowly starts to go away.

After the second pain I get scared. I know I can't stand this very long. I thought Thomas said they could do something for the pain. But no one's in the room. I'm here alone, and I'm going to die. If I have to die, I don't want it to be this painful.

The third contraction catches me by surprise, and I grit my teeth and try not to scream. I don't even feel better when the pain stops, because I know there will be more pains and they'll be worse. I try to pretend I'm somewhere else. I try to think about the home or about being outside when the air is cool and fresh, but it doesn't work. I'm not anywhere else. I'm here, and I'm going to die soon.

I think I hear somebody else screaming, someone else who's in pain too. But then I realize it's me. I feel the scream dying in my throat when the contraction ends. The scream started and stopped on its own. I wonder where it came from. Another contraction hits me, and the scream starts again, louder this time. It's making my throat sore. It's so loud that it hurts to listen to it.

The door swings open, and two nurses come in. One of them is Mrs. Potato Head. The other is smaller and mean looking.

Mean One comes up to my bed. "You're certainly making a lot of noise," she says.

I seem to have lost my voice. I can only whisper. "It hurts too much. I need something. I can't stand it."

"So childbirth hurts," Mean One says, looking at Mrs. Potato Head. "You should have thought of that sooner."

Another wave hits me, and I shut my eyes and this time the scream doesn't come back. After it's over, I feel like begging. "My doctor," I say, "my doctor said he'd give me something for the pain."

Mean One shrugs. "We'll have to see if we can find him," she says. "Only doctors can order drugs, you know." She's not in any hurry. She stands there and looks down at me.

Another contraction hits me, and then she disappears. They both do. I'm in another world of pain and bright lights. I can hear the screams again and sometimes I can feel them, but mostly I'm floating away. When I open my eyes, I can see everything whirl, even my own body. Then it all melts away until something picks me up again and hurts me. I keep trying to get away. In my mind I'm running, but the pain always catches up with me and slams me and won't let me go.

I don't know when it is that the mean nurse comes back in with Thomas. I think I see them, and then I don't, and then I can hear voices talking. I don't know if they're talking to each other or to me. Then someone's holding my arm and I can feel myself rising upward, like some kind of skyrocket bursting through the ceiling, and everything goes away and I'm not here anymore.

Sometimes I open my eyes and see people in my room, but they're in a dream. I shut my eyes or maybe I don't, and then I start to see other people. I see Jake, looking at me and holding out his hand, and I know that's wrong. It can't be. I see my mother and father and Pamela and they're looking at me too, but then they go away. I see people like LaNelle and Donna and Gracie, and they're all crying, and Rachel and Nancy and Cheryl. It seems like they all want to tell me something, but they can't.

I feel like I'm seeing my life, flipping through it like pages in a book. I run through those pages and I can't tell if I'm trying to hold on to them or tear them out. I scream, and I don't know why. I don't feel any more pain, but I scream again and again, and this time I can tell it's coming from me.

• • •

Everything looks shadowy, and my eyes ache when I try to see better. I shut them and rub them and then I can see. Thomas is in the room, and so is a nurse I haven't seen before. I rub my eyes some more and stare at them. It's dark in the room. The lamp next to my bed makes a small circle of light, but that's all.

I hear the nurse say something in a low voice, and then she leaves the room. I can hear her shoes squishing softly along the hallway.

I'm waking up a little at a time. My body hurts all over, and my head is pounding. My throat is so raw I can hardly talk. I can tell I'm not thinking clearly. Everything seems jumbled and crazy. I know where I am, but I don't know what's happened to me.

"Did I have the baby?" My voice sounds like a croak.

There's a funny hesitation in the air. I see Thomas walking closer to my bed. "How are you feeling, Anne?" he asks. "You've slept for more than a day."

"My baby," I say. "Did I have my baby?" I move my hand down my stomach. It feels loose and flabby. It reminds me of a balloon someone's let the air out of. Of course I had my baby. It's not there anymore. My body is empty. "Is my baby all right?" I ask.

Thomas looks down at his stupid clipboard. He's writing something on it. He doesn't want to look at me. "Your baby was perfectly fine," he answers, still writing.

All of a sudden I want to strangle him. How can he stand there so calmly and write? He's talking about my baby, goddammit! Why won't he look at me?

"My baby," I say. I keep repeating those words, like they're going to make a difference. "I want to know about my baby. Tell me about my baby. Stop writing whatever the hell it is you're writing. Talk to me. I have to know."

I can feel him sigh, even if I can't hear it. He lets his clipboard and pen drop to his side. "You don't want to know too much, Anne," he warns.

"Don't tell me what I want to know," I snap. It reminds me of when I heard screaming and then I realized it was coming from me. This isn't how I talk to other people. Especially not to someone like Thomas, who's been kind to me. But I don't see him as kind right now. He's a creep, like all those scummy nurses. He wants to hurt me too.

"I want to know—did I have a boy or girl?" I say. "How much did it weigh? What did it look like? When can I see it? I want to know about my baby. Don't you understand—this was my baby! You delivered it, but it was my baby. I have to know about it."

Thomas returns to his clipboard. He acts like he's reading, but I don't think he is. "You had a baby girl. She weighed eight pounds and one ounce. She was a lot bigger than I'd thought she'd be."

"I want to see her, goddammit! You can't keep me from seeing her. She's my baby, and you can't stop me. Nobody can stop me."

I start to cry because I'm so frustrated and everything hurts. I lean over and put my head on my knees. I'm howling. I haven't cried like this since I was a little girl. I can feel Thomas sit down on the edge of my bed. He pats my hair while I cry. "Cry as much as you can," I hear him say. "It's better for you to cry."

I cry until I choke and I can't cry anymore. I had a baby girl. She's been floating around in my body for almost nine months, and now she's gone. I went into the hospital with her, and now she's disappeared. She was mine and nobody else's, not even Jake's. And now she's gone. Maybe she died and they don't want to tell me.

"Is she alive?" I ask Thomas.

"She's fine, she's perfectly fine. But Anne, you know it's better if you don't see her. This way you can make a clean break."

"I don't want to make a clean break, goddammit," I shout. "You're not talking about a frigging broken arm. You're talking about my baby!"

"You've been through a lot," he says soothingly. He's trying to be kind, I know. Maybe I should be thankful for that, but I'm not. "You have to understand, you're not yourself right now."

He stands and looks down at me. "You need to sleep more, and you'll feel better later," he says. "I've ordered something that will help you sleep. We can talk about all of this tomorrow, when you're feeling more like yourself."

He leaves and a few minutes later that new nurse comes in. She isn't like the other two old crones. She looks nice and sympathetic when she sees I've been crying. "This should make you feel better," she says as she gives me a shot.

I feel more relaxed after she leaves, and I know it's from the drug. I know something else too, I think, as I fall asleep. Thomas is wrong. I'm feeling like myself now. Maybe more like myself than I've ever felt in my life.

I finally see my baby two days later. I gave up trying to persuade Thomas. All I've done is tell that dingbat social worker Mrs. Harris that I won't sign the adoption papers until I see my baby. That's what my father calls playing hardball. He used to come home sometimes and tell us how he had to play hardball with the other side. He always acted like it was something he didn't want to do, but he was pushed into it. Ha, I always thought when I looked at him. I could tell he enjoyed it. There was a funny glint in his eye.

Now I can understand how he felt. Hardball's my only choice. It's either that or never see my baby. I don't have anything to lose. And besides, it's almost fun to look Mrs. Harris in her big fish eyes and say no.

"No, I won't sign the papers until I've seen my baby," I tell her. It's the hundredth time I've said that. She's not the only one who can repeat herself until the end of time. I'm getting good at this too. She hauls out every dumb trick in her social worker's bag, yakking about things like "the good of the child" and "the good of the unwed mother" and "bonding." She talks and she talks and it doesn't make one damn bit of difference to me. I still say no.

"You can talk till the cows come home," I tell her. Maybe she'll understand that kind of country talk. "I'm not changing my mind."

"I worry about you, Anne. You're making a big, big mistake. I wish you'd listen to reason."

"Let me see my baby, and then I'll sign your goddamn papers. Don't waste your breath trying to talk me out of it."

She has some kind of mournful aura about her when she packs up and leaves, like she's doing something that hurts her terribly. "I'll arrange for it later this afternoon, and you can sign the papers in the morning," she says. "But it's against my better judgment. I hope you won't regret this, Anne."

Cheryl comes in my room later. Her room is next to mine. We're at the end of the hall so we can be separated from the other mothers. That's what the nurses call them, the other mothers. But I can tell they mean the "real" mothers. Cheryl and I aren't real.

"They're bringing my baby in soon," I tell her.

Cheryl's eyes cloud over. She gave birth to a little boy, and she signed the papers to give him up two days later. She's never seen him, and Mrs. Harris told her he's already left the hospital.

"I wish I'd done what you're doing," she says. "But they kept telling me that the sooner I signed everything and gave him up, the sooner I'd forget. If I signed the papers, then I could start a new life for myself—and for him. But the longer I waited, the worse it was going to be for both of us. Do you think I did the right thing?"

She starts to cry, and I can tell I'm about to tune up too. Ever since I had the baby, all I do is cry or get angry. It's like I don't have any other emotions. That's why I like getting angry. At least it has a little more dignity than crying.

I tell her I don't know what the right thing is. I never have. "Maybe it's better not to see your baby," I say. "I don't know. I feel like I have to, though. It's like I don't have a choice." I shrug. "Maybe this shows how nuts I am."

Cheryl has an infection, and they told her she'll have to stay in the hospital a few days longer. That doesn't seem to bother her much. I'm pretty sure I know why. I don't think she wants to leave the hospital at all. That "new life" of hers that Mrs. Harris has been babbling about isn't much of anything, as far as I can tell. She still has vague plans to go to Oklahoma City or somewhere else equally awful. Sometimes she talks about secretarial school, and sometimes she talks about going to work in a hamburger place. It sounds depressing as hell to me. It must depress her too, because she doesn't talk about it much.

We've spent the past day talking to each other. There isn't much else to do. Sometimes we sit and talk about how strange it is not to be pregnant anymore. Neither of us says it, but I think we both miss being pregnant.

That doesn't make any sense to me, because being pregnant wrecked our lives. I can't figure it out. Maybe the pregnancies ruined our lives, and then all we had left was being pregnant, and that made us like it. Or maybe it's because being pregnant is a normal state—even if being pregnant and unmarried is a terrible thing to be.

Anyway, pregnancy is normal. It's being pregnant and giving up your baby that isn't normal. It makes pregnancy look simple by comparison.

We got pregnant and wrecked our lives and started new lives at the home. Now those lives are over and we aren't pregnant any longer and our babies are gone, and we have to figure out how to put things back together.

"Just think," Cheryl says. "We'll leave here and pretend that none of this ever happened."

We hear a noise then, and both of us turn around. The nice nurse is standing in the doorway, holding a baby. She's my baby.

I forget about my stupid episiotomy stitches and how they make me walk like a duck. I almost run over to the baby. Cheryl must have left quietly, because the next thing I know I'm lying in bed, holding my baby, and the two of us are alone.

She's beautiful. She has a perfect bald head with a little bit of downy, light-colored fuzz. I bend over and kiss her on the back of her neck and she smells wonderful and sweet. I prop her against my legs and look into her eyes. They're dark blue, like Jake's, with long, dark lashes. I touch her hand, and she grasps my finger with her small, perfectly shaped fingers. I stroke her skin and look at her feet. I can't stop touching her. Then I pick her up and hold her, and I feel like I want to absorb her into my body again.

I lie back on the bed and place her on my stomach. She falls asleep there, and she breathes so quietly that I have to keep checking to see if she's still alive. She balls her hands up into fists while she sleeps. A few times she makes sucking noises.

I lie there while she sleeps, stroking her soft skin and kissing her on her sweet-smelling head. I think about how she must have come to be on a spring night when the air was warm and the breezes smelled like flowers. I didn't think of her at all then. Of course I didn't. I was so desperately in love that I couldn't think of anything else. Or maybe I wasn't in love after all. Maybe I was just desperate.

She grew inside me, starting one of those warm nights. I hated her then, when I finally realized she was there. She made me nauseated and gave me headaches. Because of her my father stopped loving me and my family sent me away. It was all so much simpler then, when I hated her. I could blame her for everything, and I could hate her and myself for ruining my life.

But she stayed with me. She grew and made a bigger place for herself, and didn't let go. I wonder if she felt me change. I wonder if she knew, somehow, that I went from hating her to loving her. I want her to know that. I want her never to forget it. I've come to love her and now I'll never stop.

I lie here and I whisper to her. I want to leave something with her so she'll remember me, but I know I can't. I tell her I love her very, very much, but I have to give her up. I want her to know I'll always be with her. I've felt her kick and push inside me, an we've been together so long that it isn't possible we'll ever be completely separate. We're a part of each other, and I'll never forget her and I'll never stop wondering where she is and how she's doing.

I look at her and try to memorize everything about her. I try to imagine how she'll look next week and next year, and how she'll grow hair and her first tooth and learn to walk and ride a bike and go to school. Will she look like me or Jake? Will she be like one of us? If I see her one day, will I recognize her or will I just keep going and never notice?

I wonder who her new parents will be and where they live and if they'll love her enough. What will they name her? What will they teach her? What will they tell her about me? I can't hate them now. I'm giving my baby to them and there's no way I can hate them. I have to try to love them. I can't think of them as taking her away from me.

They're going to be my baby's parents. I was her mother. I gave birth to her. Lying here, with her, I'm still her mother. But that's going to change forever. I won't be her mother any longer. I don't know what I'll be to her, because she won't remember me. She's about to leave me forever. She'll leave and I'll leave, and it will be as if none of this ever happened. No one will remember it but me.

I hold her close to me. When the nurse comes to pick her up, I don't cry. She's still sleeping, and I kiss her for the last time on her bald head. I watch the nurse place her in the little cart and hear the door swing shut behind them and hear the soft noises as she wheels my baby down the hall. I know those are the last sounds I'll ever hear from her, and I listen as hard as I can until I can't hear anything more.

I sign the adoption papers in the morning. Mrs. Harris brings them into my room, and two nurses come in to be witnesses. I don't bother to look at the papers or read them. I just sign my name, again and again, wherever she points. My signature gets worse and worse. After a while it looks like a line with a few humps on it. I don't care. I feel like the pen is some kind of knife and I'm using it to stab the paper. I press down harder and harder until my hand aches from the pressure, and finally I'm finished.

Mrs. Harris gathers up the papers and hands them back to me. "Don't you want to read them?" she says. "You realize how important these papers are, don't you, Anne?"

I fling the papers back at her. They fly through the air, landing everywhere. On the bed and all over the floor and on one of the chairs. I watch her pick them up slowly, one by one, and I feel bad. I don't like Mrs. Harris, but none of this is her fault. I don't know whose fault anything is anymore.

"I'm sorry," I say. "I didn't mean to do that."

She looks at me over her glasses, and her eyes are almost normal. "Are you going to be all right, Anne?" she asks. I don't answer.

"What you're doing is best for the baby," she says. "You know that. You know you're doing this for your baby. You're making the best possible decision. You're giving up your baby so she can have a better life.

"We'll place her in a wonderful, loving Christian home, Anne," she goes on. "I promise you that. She'll be loved and cherished. Her adoptive parents will be able to give her everything she needs."

I want to believe that. I want to think it's all that simple. I've tried to visualize my baby's parents, but I can only see an outline of them. The father has his arm around the mother, that's all I can tell. I try to look into that faint image I have and imagine what they're like and who they are. I want to see their faces, and look into their lives and hearts and find something that I need to know.

I know it's all useless. I've spent most of my life looking into people's faces, and in the end they haven't told me anything. It's the faces I loved best, like Jake's and my father's, that faded and disappeared from my life.

I try to imagine the kind of faces that will love and cherish my baby, but I can't see them. They stay blank. I've never seen faces like that before and I can't imagine what they'd look like.

Mrs. Landing comes to the hospital to say good-bye to Cheryl and me. She brings me a "going home" dress that my parents sent. I go into the bathroom and put it on.

It's navy blue with small red flowers and trimmed in lace, and it hangs loose from my shoulders. It looks good on me, but I feel strange to be wearing regular clothes again. I look like I used to, but everything about me is different. My episiotomy stitches hurt and my breasts ache. I had shots to make the milk dry up. But my breasts still hurt.

I come out and twirl around and try to act happy, and Cheryl and Mrs. Landing both say how pretty I am. I used to care a lot about that—about being pretty or not being as pretty as I wanted to be. It's something I haven't thought about in a long time.

"We've already shipped all your clothes and books home," Mrs. Landing tells me. "It looks like you're ready to go."

Mrs. Landing says everyone said to tell us hello. Rachel and Harriet's babies are due any day now, and they're both fine. She had a Christmas card from LaNelle, who seemed to be better, but no one's heard from Donna. She hopes Donna is all right. She still worries about her. She hasn't heard from Nancy either. "But somehow I never worry about Nancy," she says.

I start wondering again for the five hundredth time what it would be like to be Mrs. Landing. I wonder how many lives and dramas have passed through her doors, and whether she remembers most of them. For her sake I hope she has a short memory. It would be better to forget everything she's seen.

We talk about small, silly things, like how funny it is that Cheryl and I were roommates and how we went into labor at the same time. We remember the Christmas party and even the time we got drunk. Cheryl says that she's now decided definitely to go to secretarial school. She may try to see her parents too after she leaves the hospital. "It's Christmas," she says. "Maybe they'll see things differently now."

For several minutes we talk and laugh about everything except the babies we had and gave up. But when she gets up to leave, Mrs. Landing asks us how we are.

"I'm talking about how you are really," she says. "Not what you tell other people."

Cheryl's eyes fill with tears. "I think I'm getting better. I'm praying again. I'm praying a lot these days."

Mrs. Landing looks at me. Her same old look. I know I have to answer. "What about you, Anne?"

I shake my head and look at the floor. "I'm sick of people telling me I'll forget my baby," I say. "They think we can walk out of here and forget everything, don't they?"

"Some of them do," Mrs. Landing says. She hugs Cheryl, then me. "But would you want to forget your baby—even if you could?"

She leaves a few minutes later. It's a quarter till five. My father is supposed to be here to pick me up in fifteen minutes. He'll be on time, like always, and he hates for people to be late. I already have my small bag packed, and I'm ready to go. My baby's gone, and I don't belong here any longer. I don't belong where I'm going either, but I have to go anyway.

"Do you want me to come outside with you?" Cheryl asks. I say no.

We hug each other. "You're going to think this is funny," she says. "But I feel like you're the best friend I ever had."

"It's not funny," I say. "You're definitely the best friend I ever had."

The nurse makes me sit in one of those stupid wheelchairs again. She tells me it has to do with insurance. So I sit in the dumb chair in my new dress and wave goodbye to Cheryl, and the nurse wheels me down the corridor. We pass by the nursery, but the curtains are drawn and I can't see any of the babies. Thank God, I think.

I try to tell myself I should be excited to be going home and back to school and all that, but I don't feel that way. Maybe I will—when? Tomorrow? Next week? Never? Soon, I think. Any day now. I still have a long way to go if I'm going to have an optimistic personality.

Something strange happens when the elevator doors open. I ride down the corridor, but I don't see what's there. It's like the dreams I had when they drugged me up to have the baby. But I'm not drugged now. I guess I'm just crazy.

Along the hall, I feel like I can see everybody I knew at the home. They're lined up along the wall—Gracie and Donna and Nancy, looking perfect, and Rachel and Harriet, looking pious, and Cheryl and LaNelle and Thomas and Mrs. Landing. My daughter is there too, lying in a bassinet. I can't hear them say anything, but I know they're telling me good-bye. I can feel them telling me good-bye for the last time.

They're there for just a few seconds, and then the

nurse opens the outside door and pushes me through. I look back, but they're gone. I look ahead, and there's my father. He looks happy to see me. He looks me in the eyes and smiles.

"Welcome back," he says.

I stand up and he holds me at arm's length. "You look just like you always did," he says. He hugs me and gives me a kiss on the cheek.

It's cold and windy outside, and he bundles me into the car. I sit next to him, and we go spinning out of the parking lot. Driving out of town onto the open road, he reaches over and pats my hand.

"We're leaving this place behind, Anne," he says, "and we're never coming back. None of this ever happened. We're going home, and everything's going to be the same. Nothing's changed. We're still the same people we were before all of this."

He pushes harder on the gas pedal and the car roars ahead. The horizon stretches in front of us, flat and brown and hard. We're going someplace I can't see.